Gastro Detective

GASTRO DETECTIVE

A **FRANK BRUNO** NOVEL

VINCENT McCONEGHY

Patent Pending Digital • Niagara Falls, New York

 Published by Patent Pending Digital.
GastroDetective.com

Print ISBN: 978-0-615-51509-0
Kindle ISBN: 978-0-615-47507-3

First Print Edition

15 14 13 12 11 / 10 9 8 7 6 5 4 3 2 1

Edited & Formatted by Erika Q. Stokes

For Carolyna and Matthew

Food first, then morality.

Bertolt Brecht

ONE

Giuseppe Basi, known to millions of food-obsessed Americans as Chef Joe Bass (as in the string instrument, not *Micropterus salmonides*)—and he of the Food Network's *This Meal Is a Disaster Area* fame—keyed the front door to his eponymous restaurant and immediately detected the faint yet distinct odor of natural gas.

Rather than retreating, Chef entered his premises. The further he progressed through the main dining room, the more pungent the smell became.

Chefs, those who are gifted and talented, are superstitious at a minimum. Too many strange and inexplicable phenomena may be observed in the regular course of professional cheffing—maybe not so much in the production but in the consumption of food—so as to predispose them to the paranoia of bad outcomes.

Yet truly great chefs also possess abnormal sensory capabilities. Taste and palate are a given in this regard.

Chef Joe Bass also demonstrated a profound sense of smell. 'Go to the smell' was how Chef's brain worked in its native state.

Go directly to the smell.

To do so, Chef had to traverse the entire length of the front of the house before reaching the kitchen, the most likely source of the gas. He had to do this in near complete darkness since the restaurant had frosted black windows that provided sparse natural light. Located at the corner of Niagara and Portage Streets in the City of Niagara Falls, New York, it had once served as a funeral parlor belonging to the notorious Stefano Magaddino, aka Don Stefano, aka The Old Man, aka The Undertaker, blood relative of Joseph Bonanno, capo of the Bonanno crime family from New York City, and before that Castellammare del Golfo, Sicily.

From the bowels of the funeral home, Don Stefano controlled a far-reaching criminal enterprise that included most of Upstate New York, Ohio and southern Ontario; a near six-decade reign of psychopathic and folklorish terror.

His offspring, however, were neither particularly talented in organized crime nor organized mortuary sciences. The funeral home closed shortly after Don Stefano's death in 1974, and sat vacant for another two decades, before Chef Joe Bass recognized its true potential as a restaurant; a place of eating, drinking, carousing, and carrying on that was not much different from the original intent of the structure—other than everyone walked out alive at the end of the night.

Just as Don Stefano had made those doors of the funeral parlor into a romanticized destination—personally providing hammer, nails, and muscle to the coffins of so many of his deceased customers—Chef Joe Bass transformed the same bricks and mortar of this rather pedestrian fifties' ranch-style architecture into the most improbably located, Michelin single-starred restaurant in the country.

Restaurant Giuseppe Basi was not an Italian restaurant by category. It was an Italian-American restaurant and therein, along with the nostalgic back story to the former funeral home, lay the basis for the restaurant's incredible success.

Dollar for dollar, it easily out-grossed any enterprise Don Stefano ran out of the same location. Due to Chef's staggering reinterpretation of first generation Italian-American cuisine, the restaurant appealed both to locals and to the vast locust swarms of tourists that descended upon Niagara Falls during the warm months.

In other words, this meant that the left side of the menu progressed in the traditional Italian manner—*antipasti, primi, secondi, contorni, formaggi,* etc.; while the right side of the menu contained meticulously rendered versions of Chef's familial experience with American cuisine—strip steak, hamburgers, lamb chops, cold roast chicken, liver, potatoes (baked, mashed, and fried) and, of course, egg foo yung.

Chef Joe Bass was American-born, native to the city of Niagara Falls, and he understood that the average citizens of this haplessly corrupt little burg could not afford the price structure for his dishes that would yield him an appropriate margin; it was the tourists, herded and driven like cattle, who could pay the entire freight.

This was how he came upon the idea of issuing e-cards to Falls natives which entitled them to an entirely different price structure. But in order to qualify, the cardholder had to first prove what street they were born on, what grammar school they had attended, what parish they belonged to (optional), and identify how many *paesani* were also cardholders (a minimum of six required to qualify). In this manner, the restaurant remained bustling in the off-season; local cardholders also agreed to stay out of the restaurant from Memorial Day to Labor Day so that the tourists could be fleeced.

Then again, it was not just the food that garnered national and international repute for Restaurant Giuseppe Basi. It was the presence of the woman in the front of the house—Barbara Athena "Babe" La Bruna (Chef's wife)—who dressed in a black outfit every night and treated her domain with the same respect a veteran actor does the stage, even in rehearsal.

Babe La Bruna choreographed every movement and prop of the restaurant, allowing Chef to turn his back to his customers and concentrate on the food; to make the food he had first served Babe when they were teenagers; the food that mesmerized and dazzled all for its sheer simplicity and structure; the food that might seem far beneath a chef of Joe Bass's technical expertise and stature; the food first identified by blogger Hayden

Buckingham as the truest expression of the Italian-American idiom; the food that seduced Babe in the back seat of Chef's 1978 Chevrolet Camaro in a desolate parking lot, producing their first and only pregnancy which was quickly aborted; the food that ultimately was sourced from the kitchen of Maria Grazia San Lorenzo, the woman Chef had grown up calling Nona (when in reality she was his landlord), and who allowed young Giuseppe Basi to stand by her side as a little boy, watching her cook, and in doing so, imparted the one and only encounter Chef had with unconditional love.

The smell of gas is a harbinger of danger; quite ingenious, really, since it is not the gas itself (methane, CH_4) that smells but the introduction of a second gas, methanethiol (CH_3SH), which provides the stink. Chef learned the organic nature of this compound during an early material safety handling class at Trott Vocational High School, home to the mechanically gifted yet hopelessly undiagnosed dyslexic students of his generation in the public school system of the seventies.

Chef remembered that hard, take-away lesson when confronted by the smell of methanethiol that was burned into him by his metal shop teacher—the one with the mutton chop sideburns, arm tattoos from Vietnam, and a three-pack-a-day cigarette habit (all smoked while in class).

VENTILATE.

Chef fumbled through the darkness toward his kitchen; the exhaust fan would have normally been set to run all night to vent the cooking line but in January there was no need for such a precaution. Chef caught his right, ingrown big toe on the corner of table 39 and howled like wounded animal.

He hopped his entire weight onto his left foot, took two stuttering steps forward, and crumpled under his girth, banging his head on table 43. The force of the fall rendered Chef unconscious by the time he reached the floor in semi-concussed blackness, further enhanced by the methanethiol.

The gas multiplied and seeped into the basement.

Chef did not regain consciousness until his cousin, Leonard Krolewski, the restaurant's porter and roundsman, came to his aid nearly forty minutes later. Cousin Leonard possessed no sense of smell or taste whatsoever. He was also one of those severely dyslexic graduates of the vocational educational system but capable of repairing most anything electrical or mechanical within the confines of the restaurant, certifying him as an ideal and trustworthy candidate to carry the only other key cut to open the kitchen door.

Not even Babe had a key to the kitchen. Not in a million years.

"What happened, Chef?" Cousin Leonard asked.

Chef sat up groggily, while the smell of methanethiol jolted him to the present.

"Jesus H. Christ, you didn't turn on the lights, did you?"

"No; I came through the front door like you must have. I nearly tripped over you on my way to take a piss."

"You don't smell that, do you?"

"You know I can't smell nothing, Chef, on 'count of my accident."

"This place is full of gas. And it's about to blow if we don't ventilate and find out where it's coming from."

"Why don't we call the fire department?"

"Fuck that, those whores," Chef said, standing up. "It's got to be from the kitchen. Who closed last night?"

"Same as always—Bobo, Jason, and Pops. And your wife."

"Whose cock was she sucking? Bobo's?"

Cousin Leonard frowned. "Don't talk about your wife that way, Chef."

"She likes black cock, doesn't she?"

Cousin Leonard refused to answer.

"The answer is no, Leonard," Chef said, now on his feet and wobbly. "She doesn't like any cock. She likes pussy."

"We all know that," Cousin Leonard said.

"Yes, we do. Those dimwits must have left a burner on or something. Go open the kitchen door and don't turn anything on, especially the lights."

Cousin Leonard obeyed Chef's command.

Chef made his way into the kitchen, and when the light from the outside crept in as the kitchen door opened just enough to help him to navigate in the darkness, he could not believe what he saw. There, in the full open position, were burners number four and seven on the Vulcan eight-burner stove, their pilot lights fully extinguished.

Could his dishwasher have carelessly bumped the control valves of the stove while mopping the kitchen floor up last night before close? One burner, perhaps…? He had seen that happen before... but two?

Chef grabbed a broomstick and told Cousin Leonard to get outside the kitchen immediately. He turned the burners off and then reached for the switch to the ANSUL system mounted high on the kitchen exhaust hood. He was half in the kitchen and half out; he figured if it blew he would be propelled into a snow bank and the insurance money and business interruption policy coverage would cover everything else.

At some point in time, even the most wildly successful chef wants out—by any means necessary—of the place that bore him his greatest success. And only then, when everything is lost, sold, bartered, or bankrupt, does a chef realize he wants back in.

"I'm tripping the switch to the exhaust, Leonard," Chef said. "If it blows we'll meet again in the galley of the *Edmund Fitzgerald* at the bottom of Lake Superior."

The belt-driven fan at the top of the exhaust stack kicked in. There was a rush of air through the filters, the back door nearly pulled shut from the negative vibe of the fan; and the poorly designed make-up air system, implemented by Chef's cousin, Domenic "shit-for-brains" Basi, spit forth the first breath of freshly returned oxygen.

Venting accomplished. They would live to cook another day at Restaurant Giuseppe Basi.

"Now who the fuck did this?" Chef demanded that Leonard participate in a chef's second occupation—that of speculating as to the maneuverings and wheelings-and-dealings of his employees and his colleagues in the restaurant business.

"It had to be Lo Piccolo. He's been trying to take you out for years. He's very jealous of you, Chef."

"You don't think it was the dishwasher? I can see one burner being left on, but two? This is just plain retarded."

"Lo Piccolo's father was a low-lifer from the West Side of Buffalo and a bag man for Freddie Lupo. You know he memorizes every line of dialog from *One, Two* and *Goodfellas,* don't you?"

"I've heard that. His restaurant," Chef Joe Bass smiled and posed, as if on mark at his recently canceled show for the Food Network, "is a complete Disaster Area."

"When that chick-writer came to town and she did that piece about you in the newspapers, he was all upset about that."

"Hayden Buckingham?"

"Yeah, your little preppy cooze with the big words. That set him off again."

"Well, you schmooze, you cooze."

"Big time. And you got that national TV show, those endorsement deals, and you did all that from this god-forsaken place. I mean even Buffalo looks down on the city of Niagara Falls. It's the single most ass-backwards place in America."

"It's not even a part of America, Leonard. Our fair city is a suburb of Palermo. Tell me more about Bebe Lo Piccolo. This is interesting. What the fuck kind of name is Bebe?"

"He's a camel jockey—Lebanese. You married Babe. He's been trying to get at her for decades."

"He didn't get the memo about her muff diving? No, I suppose not. That's just for you and me, now isn't it, you Polack?"

"I know that."

"Yes, but for Lo Piccolo to even consider me his competition is just plain absurd. He does weddings. His joint looks like a Puerto Rican mausoleum. He puts pork in his meatballs. How tragic is that?"

"You do owe him money, Chef."

"Yes I do," Chef Joe Bass nodded. "But that's almost all taken care of. The show going dark caught me by surprise. I'm still on contract. I'm bigger than Emeril and if they decide to fuck me off like they did him, it's no hair off my balls. I'll just land somewhere else."

"I'd get him paid off sooner than later. You still banging that cooze?"

"Who?"

"Buckingham."

"Oh, no, no, no. I'm way too toxic for her. I'm so mid-naughts and besides, now she's a star."

"What do you mean?"

"She's a star, Leonard. You can't read. The woman is all over the television and the Internet. She has a three-book deal, a movie coming out next year—some documentary about eating and banging within a hundred miles of your crapper—and she's crusading for local produce in school systems. She also has a big secret."

"A secret?"

"Yes, she still eats meat."

"No kidding."

"Yes, sir. I pulled a pebble out of her ass just the other night in New York. From the perfume of the specimen, I'd guess that she's been dining on locally raised, organic, free range chicken vindaloo."

"But you said…"

"I said I wasn't banging her. I didn't say I wasn't sodomizing her. Big difference."

"I'll get the tomatoes," Cousin Leonard said. "Chef, where is Palermo? Is it in Ohio?"

"Yeah, it's right next to Parma," Chef Joe Bass replied, firing a snowball at Cousin Leonard. "It's back to work for us working men. We've got one-fifty on the books tonight. My head is killing me. I think I have a concussion."

TWO

From the moment Restaurant Giuseppe Basi first opened its doors, only Cousin Leonard and Chef completed the necessary prep work to ready the kitchen for dinner service. The restaurant did not serve lunch and remained closed on Sundays. Prep hours generally ran from eight in the morning until three in the afternoon, followed by a staff meal at four o'clock when discussions of the upcoming evening took place in a cascading order of importance. There was hardly ever mention of the food. There was no need. The food never changed.

Cousin Leonard began his employment devoid of any cooking experience or preconceived notions of food, other than it provided him fuel to walk, talk, and set his fishing line in the water. Chef recognized these traits as a superior pedigree to create a zombie roundsman capable of producing gallons of chicken stock, brodo di carne, minestra, brodo di pesce, salsa di pomodoro, ragù al coniglio, meatloaf, buttermilk mashed potatoes, zuppa alla stracciatella, pasta e fagioli, lentils, peas and rice, and meatballs whose protein source came solely from veal and egg.

That was just the beginning of it.

There was fresh pasta that had to be produced daily—fusillia alla calabrese, tornarelli for the cacio e pepe, lasagnette for the San Giuseppe (Chef's namesake saint and specialty of the house), gnocchi di ricotta, gnocchi di patate, and ravioli.

Basta.

Then steaks had to be cut by hand. Lamb shanks, too. Vegetables must be rinsed, soaked, cleaned, and lightly cooked for the antipasti table. Burgers must be ground fresh each day. Bread—don't forget the bread—an extremely wet dough mixed to 80% hydration and left to rise overnight in the walk-in cooler before it was cut, proofed and baked in the pizza oven at two p.m.

Then there was the famous house green salad composed of seventy percent iceberg lettuce, ten percent curly endive, ten percent torn spinach leaves, and the remainder chopped romaine. The dressing was two parts Filippo Berio olive oil (not some expensive extra virgin variety) to one part cheap apple cider vinegar. And spices (undisclosed).

With the exception of the chicken stock, garlic and onions were forbidden in almost all recipes by direct order of Chef. This was how he had learned to cook from Maria Grazia San Lorenzo, who shared his abnormal sense of smell, only more so in that these two ingredients—the mere aroma of their release—had made her physically ill and so her cooking called for their use sparingly.

Fresh herbs were also frowned upon (an unnecessary expense) with the exception of basil. Maria Grazia San Lorenzo made do without them, reasoned Chef, and so should he. Just because something is available does not mean that it should be used. Nothing irritated Chef Joe Bass more than seeing fresh herbs used as a garnish on the plate without any relation to the underlying preparation.

There were three dairy products manufactured in-house on a consistent basis—butter, mozzarella, and ricotta. Milk, eggs, and chickens arrived from a local farmer, from an undisclosed location (secretaries of defense guard their launch codes, chefs guard their farmer sources).

Chicken was also treated rather oddly in Chef's kitchen. He roasted the whole bird, then let it sit for a day wrapped in the cooler, split it, and served the halves cold on a plate with sliced tomatoes, cucumbers, and sliced potatoes. He decided upon this method because he concluded that it was impossible to roast a whole chicken to order in a satisfactory manner—with the small kitchen staff he maintained—without rendering the fowl dry. But serving the chicken cold bypassed this complication. It was that very dryness of the protein that Chef sought; a state that allowed the salting of the cold pieces to re-awaken on the palate. The dish resided on the American side of the menu—Leftover Cold Chicken Platter—and was a consistent best seller.

Certain vegetables, in season, came from the same farmer. But that was the extent to which Chef embraced the current locally-raised, locally-sourced, locally-hyped food craze. He was more interested in paying cash to his vendors in order to avoid his locally-born state sales tax auditor. Credit cards were a fact of life in the restaurant business, especially with the overwhelming touristy majority of his customers. So there was very little cash at the end of the day for him to squirrel away, or so he thought, since he never counted the money anyways.

That was Babe's job. Chef Joe Bass was bad with money.

But the state had also clamped down from the vendor side on restaurants that paid cash for their provisions, auditing both suppliers and customers; so whatever cash purchases Chef did make, he tendered them to farmers who would no more turn him into the state than surrender one square inch of their land to the Federal government.

We have neglected to mention tripe.

It was not on the original menu of Restaurant Giuseppe Basi but when Chef's mother, Gloria, came into the restaurant informing him that she needed double aortic aneurysm surgery, she asked her son if he would prepare Maria Grazia's tripe to calm her nerves. The next day Gloria ate the tripe. The following day she had the surgery, coded twice on the operating table, caught sepsis in the ICU, and regained consciousness thirty days later, Chef at her side.

Gloria credited the tripe with saving her life, not the skill of the surgeon or the care she had received in the ICU, but the recurring vision of her eating tripe in her son's restaurant that brought her back to the land of the living.

Tripe went on the menu for good at Restaurant Giuseppe Basi.

The matter of desserts and *dolci* spawned one of only two arguments about the menu between Chef and Babe. Chef was adamant in his desire to provide neither a dessert course nor coffee service. Chocolate, sugar—the pastry arts in general—were simply not in Chef's lexicon, although he had suffered through the necessary course work at his community college's culinary arts program. He was rather offended at his wife's insistence that something had to occupy this part of the service, so a grand compromise was arranged.

Customers would not be presented with dessert options tableside. Instead, they would be directed to the espresso bar that was built adjacent to the regular bar, where they had a choice of cannoli or sfogliatelle and hand-pulled espresso. The cannoli shells were made from a recipe of verified Sicilian origin (as in Cefalù from the hand scribbled notes of Donna DiStefano-Guercio, a distant relative and bona fide witch); while the house-made ricotta and candied citrus formed the basis of the interior of the cannolis.

The sfogliatelle was Chef's grandest homage to

Maria Grazia San Lorenzo. It took him a full calendar year to perfect the technique of the pasta frolla, spun into the intricate clam shape layer upon layer, and train Cousin Leonard in the process. When a test a version of the sfogliatelle finally came out of the convection oven to his satisfaction—just enough crunch at the triangular tips—Chef broke down and wept that Maria Grazia was dead and long gone and could not be here to taste them with him.

The other matter of compromise between Chef and Babe was a bit more severe.

"Why don't you make a Bolognese?" Babe inquired while dipping the ends of bread into a bowl of sauce. Babe ate little other than bread and sauce.

"Bolognese? That's what you call your mother's meat sauce?"

"No I don't," Babe said, sensing she had stepped into a deep patch of doodoo. "It's just that I'm starting to see it on menus more often. You know, on some the white-tablecloth places up in Buffalo and when we travel around to New York."

"I see it too, Babe. Guess what I see when I see it on someone else's menu? I see a Disaster Area."

Babe rolled her eyes. Here we go again, she thought.

"Let's think about it, shall we," Chef Joe Bass could not let this moment pass. "We would have to make tagliatelle. It took me six months to train Cousin Leonard on tornarelli. We would have to buy the proper die to extrude the pasta, and not just any old die: we need the one that would extrude it to the exact specifications as set forth in City Hall, in bronze, in Bologna. The last thing I need is for some Italian tourist coming in here and pulling me over to his table to lecture me on how this is not a true rendition of *Tagliatelle Bolognese.*"

"OK, let's just forget I even mentioned it."

"No, we are not going to forget it. Think about what you just asked me. We would have to add milk to make the sauce. When have we ever added milk to our sauce? I would have to add wine to the sauce, also. This is like asking a Hasidim Jew to sit down to a plate of bangers and mash. It is against my very *existence.* Maria Grazia would never put wine in any sauce with tomatoes. Whatever wine we could afford—and it was rare indeed to have wine, since she was allergic to it—was served on the table and consumed in a glass. Not put into some bullshit sauce from the North."

"You act as if Maria Grazia was your own blood. She was not. She rented the cottage house in the back to your family. It was a dump; I've seen it."

"Oh, yes, of course. And I am adopted as well. Probably not even one drop of true Italian *sangue* running through my veins. But let's get back to Bolognese, shall we?"

"Let's not. You're freaking me out."

"Then to really be true to it—so again the Italians don't complain too much when they are bussed in here on their packaged deals—I would have make it with organ meat. Offal. Now every Tom, Dick, and Sally who has eaten Bolognese in all those nice white-tablecloth restaurants you cited in starting this discussion would complain: 'This isn't the Bolognese I'm used to. It's very different.' Who needs that shit?"

"I'm done," Babe said. "I'm going to do the deposit."

Babe handled all the money. This was something else that was discussed once and then never again.

"You want a meat sauce. A *ragù*. Just like your Mother's," Chef could not resist the jab.

"I'm so over this conversation."

"Yes, with onions and garlic in the sauce, stinking up the kitchen just like your Mother's kitchen used to stink. You said so yourself the first time I brought you to dinner at Maria Grazia's. You said: "Oh, my god, I've never tasted food like this. It's so light. It's soooo light!"

"How many times did you look up Maria Grazia's skirt when you were a little boy standing next to her in the kitchen?"

"So predictable and wrongheaded, Babe. You just can't admit what a heinous cook your Mother was."

"I'll admit to marrying you solely on the basis of your anticipated sperm donation which turned out to be a bust, anyways. There were no infertility doctors in Niagara Falls in the eighties, unless you count those Pakistani butchers."

Right there, Chef pulled back on the subject matter of infertility. It was his kryptonite; actually, it was a shared burden between them. The tests were inconclusive, pointing to problems in both directions. They went about their separate ways; Babe counting the money while Chef prepped for service.

Rigatoni al ragù made it onto the menu a few weeks later after an utter and complete silence transpired between Chef and Babe. He called Babe one day and invited her in for lunch, something they used to do in the early days of the restaurant. He served her the rigatoni (Babe's favorite dry pasta), grated the cheese over the plate just to her liking (a Sardinian sheep's milk variety), and poured her a glass of Amarone.

But please, he begged her, never again ask him to make something that might expose him to criticism or ridicule from the Italians. This was an Italian-American restaurant, built from the same limited resources and stretched pantry of the products available to Maria Grazia when she first immigrated to America in the year 1929. They made do in those days with a very different ingredient set then and Restaurant Giuseppe Basi would make do in the same way now. The Japanese may have the most evolved sense of language when explaining taste, he told Babe, with their elaborate nomenclature for sensory descriptors such as *umami,* but we, he said, we only have one thing—*cucina casareccia.*

This is our house. We only make what we know.

Cousin Leonard brought a case's worth of number-ten cans of plum tomatoes in a ghetto-rigged grocery-shopping cart back to the kitchen from the basement. Chef waited for them to begin his work in the exact same manner he did with most prep shifts—salsa di pomodoro, first.

Even when he was away from the restaurant in New York, shooting *Disaster Area* for Food Network, he was never gone long enough to miss more than several rotations of batches of salsa di pomodoro. Cousin Leonard had been trained in its preparation but still had a tendency to over-process it. He worried about being away for too long for precisely this reason.

That was the thing about having a national cooking show: The money was not so great (at least that's what everyone told him) but the endorsement deals that resulted from the exposure were where Chef Joe Bass planned to cash in.

In fact, the extra money from his show was manna from heaven. There was nothing in the way of extra income that Chef Joe Bass would ever turn down or thumb his nose up at.

It was gravy.

The cans of tomatoes Cousin Leonard brought him had been stripped of their labels, a precautionary food-service practice of secrecy that Chef instituted from day one to arrest any interlopers or curiosity seekers in his pantry. Nothing in a can or box carried a label in Chef Joe Bass's kitchen. He and Cousin Leonard alone knew the products' origins, vendor codes, and sell-by dates.

He often received shipments of canned goods from exotic locations from his "cousin," Frank Bruno, the maternal grandson of Maria Grazia San Lorenzo, who was also a formally trained chef—a graduate of the

CIA, the Culinary Institute of America. Chef considered him a brother.

They had grown up together in the alleyway that backstopped the cottage house and the main house on 6th Street in Niagara Falls. Their daily interactions were unrestricted and interchangeable throughout the years of childhood and adolescence. They walked to school together. They played stickball and street hockey in the alley. They earned money organizing deliveries for the neighborhood bakery by way of a legion of homeless men who transported bread in their bicycles throughout the city, collecting pennies per loaf for their logistical maneuverings.

But when it came time for dinner, future Chef Joe Bass remained at Maria Grazia's side as her personal sous chef. Frank Bruno, on the other hand, dressed in a clean white shirt, put a linen napkin over his arm, and played the role of maitre d'. He was destined for the front of the house, or so everyone thought when they all came together for Sunday dinner, or for leftovers of Sunday dinner throughout the remainder of the week.

Now Frank sent Chef all sorts of canned and bottled products from Israel, Russia, Kazakhstan, Peru, Italy, Djibouti, Yemen, Qatar, and El Salvador. No one really knew quite what Frank Bruno did for a living, other than his official explanation that he was a GS-15 employee of the Federal Government contracted to run the foodservice operations at American embassies abroad.

The products Frank sent usually arrived by air transport via the Air Force's 914th Tactical Airlift Unit

Command that was based at the Niagara Falls airport. Someone from the base delivered them to Chef's kitchen back door in exchange for gift certificates or a free dinner. A very few of the products were hits, like the Israeli olive oil or the Greek feta, while others Chef had no use for other than to indulge his culinary curiosity, as in those from the Middle East, Africa, and Asia.

The only indispensable product sent to him by Frank Bruno, the one he salivated over while opening the box, were of course his prized canned tomatoes and the *colatura di alici,* the amber juice extracted from anchovies off the Amalfi coast and aged in chestnut barrels before bottling.

This was the secret ingredient in Chef's spaghetti alle vongole, his minestra di zucchini, and his linguine al prezzemolo. But it was not included in his pasta e fagoli. That was an even more closely guarded secret by Chef and Cousin Leonard, held with the same form of zealotry exhibited by the Coca-Cola Corporation of Atlanta, Georgia, over their fizzy soda pop.

Chef Joe Bass popped three ibuprofen from a small container of pills and vitamins he carried with him and took the tomatoes out of the shopping cart. Cousin Leonard went downstairs to cut steaks, grind burgers, open clams for the clams casino, and filet a shipment of pompano that had just arrived fresh from the fish monger.

Chef's head throbbed from his fall this morning and his near methanethiol asphyxiation. He played injured. Everyone played injured in the restaurant business. That's just the way things were done. There were no such thing as sick days.

That's when Babe La Bruna popped her head into the kitchen—dressed, of course, in full black apparel—this time an Athletica sweatsuit. She was stunning. No matter what Babe wore, her beauty conveyed itself in a way that someday will all be very well understood and represented in scientific journals by a precise sequence of genetic markers. She was a feminine version of her father, Carmine La Bruna, a beautiful man to whom other men capitulated in the pursuit of pussy. Sloppy seconds off of Carmine La Bruna qualified for lifetime achievement in many a cocksman's curriculum vitae.

"Leonard told me what happened. Are you OK? Let me see your head," Babe reached up to touch Chef's eyebrow.

"That stings. I feel like shit."

"Go home. Go to bed."

"Not with a hundred fifty on the books."

"Can't we hire someone to help out? It's ridiculous for you to work these hours. You've been on a top-rated national television show and here you are working like a dog."

"Been. I've *been* on a national television show. Hell, I've hawked macaroni and cheese for Kraft. But not anymore. Nobody will touch me right now."

"Well, you did use profanity on *Larry King.*"

Chef had been summoned as a last minute substitute stand-in for Emeril LaGasse in a panel discussion on the *Larry King* television show. The guests included Michael Pollan, author of the *Omnivore's Dilemma,* Barbara Kingsolver of *Animal Vegetable, Miracle,* Alice Waters of *Chez Panisse,* and—wink, wink—Chef Joe Bass for his everyday, rough-and-tumble rapport with grossly obese America.

The episode was spurred on by a national incidence of *E. coli* infestation of ground beef in several fast food chains. Shots of dead or dying Taco Bell customers opened the segment with Larry King's hack Sir Lawrence Olivier impersonation providing the segue— *'Iz it Safe? Iz our food supply safe? Do you visk your life when you go out to eat a hamburger? We'll be back in just a moment with our special guest panel of experts….'*

They took Chef Joe Bass's video interview from a local broadcast affiliate in Buffalo. He appeared Nixon-sweaty because he had just finished putting out a banquet for one hundred people and he had raced over to the TV studio. His audio feed was terribly over-modulated, making it nearly impossible for him to hear the producer's cue. None of that mattered. To this day, Chef still did not understand the basic premise of the topic.

"What about you, Chef Joe Bass," Larry King had said, "do you agree with our guests that our national food supply chain is horribly broken?"

Silence.

Chef Joe Bass's trajectory to fame and national persona was an improbable quirk in the time-space food-service continuum. His thoughts were not. They were wholly his own.

"Larry, I believe that your guests are mentally ill."

"Whoa, hold on a moment, Chef," Larry said.

"What you see and what you read from people like this is mostly pathological narcissism."

"Now wait just a moment," Alice Walters's sexless voice rose up.

Who could have ever banged such a dead fish? Chef thought. "OK, Larry, let me put it to you another way," he said. "They're all full of shit."

Cut to commercial.

It had made it out onto the air. It made its way to the front page of the *New York Post,* to the food blogs of the *New York Times,* to every trade magazine and website in the food business. National political commentators weighed in. It was an epochal moment—a clash of the cultures—a red state/blue state issue and a lesson in food and politics.

Hayden Buckingham produced the most scathing headline in her blog when she declared Chef Joe Bass *A Disaster Area All Unto Himself.* She went on to suggest that Chef crawl back under the rock she had unearthed him from nearly five years ago and hopefully never be heard from again.

The *National Enquirer* linked Chef Joe Bass to Whitney Houston's cocaine problem. Not surprisingly, this was the only bit of press that actually seemed to upset his mother, Gloria. Chef had the issue framed in his kitchen office cubbyhole; he was so proud and honored to be on the cover of the Enquirer. He was finally starting to realize, in the midst of the great public controversy generated by his one profane tirade on national television, his greatest love of all—himself.

Thank you, Whitney Houston.

No one else in television loved Chef Joe Bass after that appearance. The Food Network cancelled *Disaster Area* but after much back and forth between attorneys, agreed to keep him under contract for the final six months if he did, indeed, do what Hayden Buckingham suggested and crawl back on his hands and knees under the rock he climbed out of—Niagara Falls, New York.

"Who would have left the burners running on the stove?" Babe asked her husband. "Who dished last night?"

"It's kinda funny, if it wasn't a coincidence and this is how someone decided to blow up the place up. Only in Niagara Falls. Maybe it was Lo Piccolo."

"How did they get in?"

"Who's they?"

"I don't know."

"Maybe 'they' is one of us."

"The crew?"

"I'm just saying."

"Impossible. You owe him money, don't you?"

"Who, Lo Piccolo? Just a little friendly wagering. It's my money, no need to be concerned."

"It's *our* restaurant, moron."

"Where to, today, yogalates?"

"I'm going shooting with Krista at the range. I'm getting my permit to carry. I really don't like this neighborhood at night. It's a war zone during the day but at least you can see things. And I can't rely on Pops walking me to my car. He's fifty-nine years old. I think he has cancer. Have you seen the way he's been hacking his lungs out lately?"

"I've seen it. It's not good. OK, little sure-shot. Move along now. I have work to do. See you at four for staff meal."

"See you then."

Ah, the magical, relationship enhancing qualities of reverse work schedules. Chef worked days, prepping, and nights only on special occasions. Babe worked every night until close.

"I'm going to do the deposit," Babe said.

"Go get 'em little Annie Oakley. I love you."

"Et tu, Brute."

Now, finally alone in his kitchen, Chef turned to the task at hand and began opening the number ten cans of plum tomatoes. He emptied the contents into a twenty-gallon stockpot and blended the tomatoes with the assistance of a burr mixer. He muscled the pot onto the stove, eyeballed a quantity of salt, basil, and olive oil, and set the pot to flame.

That was it.

There was nothing more to Restaurant Giuseppe Basi's rendition of salsa di pomodoro, other than a thirty minute reduction followed by a rapid chill and a reheat to order. There was no secret. That was the secret. The secret was to restrain the impulse to add or do anything else to the recipe. In this matter, all discussion was finished. The heroic part of its preparation came from the radical notion that nothing else could or should be added to it.

But there were other matters to ponder, if not ingredients to add, to this moment alone with the salsa di pomodoro for Chef Joe Bass.

What if Hayden Buckingham had not stumbled into his place five years ago while on assignment by the *New York Times* to write a tchotchke send-up of those couples that still honeymoon at Niagara Falls?

What if he had hesitated and did not lay that line of bullshit on her about how he was bound and determined to heed the call of Paul Bocuse and not die drunk on his feet like all the countless chefs before them, staggering into kitchen oblivion?

Lucky for him, Hayden Buckingham had grown up on Connecticut prep school and country club food so that she would swallow such a line of bullshit. Lucky for Chef Joe Bass that Hayden Buckingham swallowed it all. She was brutally cunning, correctly identifying food as *the* issue of the next decade and beyond. But she needed an exemplar to strut her muscular prose and there stood Chef Joe Bass, all 245 pounds of unabridged testosterone.

What did the Food Network executives say after the Larry King fiasco? 'We've got Guy Fieri now. Emeril's long gone, forgotten. He's our red state guy. You were always just a bit too Northeastern and ethnic if you read the demographics carefully. Now, if you were Hispanic, you could have fucked Alice Waters backwards on national TV and we'd have doubled your contract. You just declared your last Disaster Area. Don't even think about using that title. We own it.'

Chef Joe Bass did not have a whole lot to show for his three years of celebrity. Babe controlled all of the money. She controlled the sex, or in Chef's orthodoxy, the fact that she had begun acting on long-repressed desires and started sleeping with other women, she controlled the sex that really mattered. His dalliances with other women were old school, shoot 'em up, bang-bang incidents, except for his on-again, off-again tryst with Hayden Buckingham. That chick had gotten into his head.

Chef controlled nothing except the execution of the salsa di pomodoro and that was something even an idiot, such as Cousin Leonard—because he was an idiot and would not stray one iota from the mandated recipe—could accomplish.

The sauce came to boil and Chef promptly lowered

the heat. He grabbed another stockpot to prepare brodo di carne and walked it into the cooler. His head started to throb again.

Maybe he should go lay down for a bit on the office couch?

Cousin Leonard could handle the rest, he thought. He always did without complaint just so long as he was paid in cash by three o'clock on Tuesday afternoon. This method of compensation did not conflict with Cousin Leonard's social security disability payments, welfare check, and veteran's pension. Cousin Leonard was a borderline moron with an I.Q. Wechsler score of 72 but he was no dummy in matters of governmental compensation. He knew how the game was played.

Chef opened the walk-in door and gathered the celery, beef bones, carrots, and parsley to begin the brodo. He was not making beef stock in the classic sense where the bones would be roasted before being immersed in liquid. This was one of his favorite preparations and something Maria Grazia used as the base in most of her soups. When he read a formal recipe of it in a Marcella Hazan cookbook, with an explanation that it was put there at the insistence of her husband, Victor, Chef knew that his vision for Restaurant Giuseppe Basi was the correct one—*cucina casareccia.*

But it was a bad location for a kitchen walk-in cooler. It had been placed there for Chef's convenience, not as a well-designed position for a heavily foot-trafficked area, and it opened onto the blindside of the server return. Thousands of dollars in inventory had to be pitched into the trash over the years based solely upon the ill-conceived placement of that walk-in and the resultant kitchen collisions that it had produced.

This was a different type of collision. The boning knife went in just under Chef's rib cage and pierced the proximal (closest to the point of origin) portion of the left anterior descending coronary artery—the widow maker. That incision alone would have been enough to guarantee the demise of Chef Joe Bass, but the knife went further into the ventricle, a few more centimeters, hastening the rupture in tissue and creating a catastrophic hemorrhage whose crimson presence quickly engulfed the clean, pressed whites of his chef's coat. The shade of red closest to death was a much different hue from the salsa di pomodoro now simmering on the stove.

THREE

The BMW sedan under full escort by the *Carabinieri*—the Italian national police—pulled out from the side entrance of the American embassy in Rome onto Via Boncompagni before turning onto Via Vittorio Veneto. The driver, for reasons unfathomable to Frank Bruno, sitting in the rear seat next the American ambassador, plugged an address into his GPS; a sign that perhaps this plainclothes Marine had been in Italy for too long and had turned native.

Italians are boundless in their infatuation for the latest digital devices. They were Europe's most fervent early adopters of cell phones and their propensity to build cell phone towers had transformed the nation, allowing for crystal clear reception in even the most remote mountaintop villages, where copper cable and modern plumbing had never been fully implemented.

Wireless technology had conquered what Hannibal could only dream of when he crossed the mountains into Calabria: providing connectivity from Basilicata to the Brenner Pass. Now it was possible for the chronically unemployable to move out of the South without drama and go seek work wherever the modern economy might take them, while still having a clear dial tone to the most important character actor in the modern Italian nation-state—Mama.

Frank made a quick mental note to keep his eye on the driver. It was not as if any GPS inputs were required to navigate their vehicle to the Vatican, not with the garish escort provided by the Carabinieri. Then again, maybe the Marine was doing something so routine and so out of the realm of his obsessive paranoia that Frank decided to let the moment pass without comment and stare out the window to the great show the Carabinieri was about to perform.

Long before he had been trained to observe such things professionally, Frank Bruno understood his innate ability to store and retrieve the idiosyncratic gestures of other people. His mind worked at the boundaries of eidetic memory. Man had evolved. Frank accepted this premise. But each man, each woman, had evolved in a peculiar way and this tenaciously guarded sentiment, more than anything else, formed the basis of his belief system.

Take, for example, the man sitting next to him, the American ambassador to Italy, Melvin Philip Reed. The first time Frank met Reed was twenty years earlier in

Washington, D.C., at the State Department. Reed was set to become the U.S. Ambassador to the nascent Republic of Croatia, and he was participating in a three-day intensive orientation after securing his position through a vast amount of fundraising he had accomplished on behalf of George Herbert Walker Bush.

Frank had been a junior member of a CIA team invited in by the State to provide a fifty thousand foot regional threat analysis to the new crop of "emerging democracy" ambassadors and the thing that stood out about Reed then was the same thing that struck Frank now in the backseat of the BMW—he suffered from an excessive amount of nostril hair protrusion and a sardonic yet endearing laugh.

You do not become Ambassador to Italy with chronic nostril hair protrusion unless you have interests above and beyond those of the United States of America.

Frank made a note.

But he liked Reed, or at least he determined he could work with Reed on this given assignment, which was not the case with the asshole sitting in the front seat of the BMW, the Charge d'affaires, Hairston Milbrand III. Milbrand was a Yale graduate like Reed, but that was about all the two shared in common.

Milbrand defined the archetypal career Foreign Service Officer (FSO or faggot service officer, technical term). Open in his hostility to Frank, Milbrand went a step further, in Frank Bruno's opinion, when he had alerted the U.S. Ambassador to the Holy See, Hector

Ortiz, of the meeting that the American embassy had been directed to arrange at the Vatican with the most senior members of the Church.

The last time Frank was in town to meet with a Pope was in the very early days of the Boston priest sex-abuse scandal, back in 1996 to be exact. That meeting with John Paul II did not go very well either, and nearly ended in a fist fight between Frank and Raymond Flynn, the then United States Ambassador to the Holy See.

Flynn was shocked by the brazen and unpolished manner in which a mid-level CIA operative, such as Frank, had been chosen to address the Pope's closest advisers on this developing situation. His two-minute synopsis of the impending crisis of priest sexual abuse was utterly graphic in detail and lacking any true diplomatic competency.

Frank remembered Flynn recoiling at his use of some terms in his analysis but this was a carefully choreographed strategy designed to obliterate the protecttorate of diplomatic language and hopefully shock the Church into taking action. He did what he came to do and that was to utter the phrase "rim job" in front of John Paul II. The expression had actually made it into translation in Polish, back to the Pontiff, before the room erupted in chaos.

Maybe it wasn't such a good idea to have a young CIA operative address the Pope.

"I ought to take you out back and kick the fuck out of you," Flynn had told Frank.

Frank had sized up Flynn; he probably could have landed some shots before Bruno eventually took him down. The opportunity to speak before Pope John Paul II, however, was a deeply personal matter. As a former captain of the altar boys of his local parish, and twelve-year product of a Catholic school education, Frank remembered distinctly how it all went down.

Father Walter Judd was a jovial priest, liked and respected by all for the breath of fresh air he had injected into the sagging parish of St. Mary of the Cataract Church. He attended the boy's grammar school basketball practices and was always present in the locker room, doling out encouragement before and after games. He even took several boys out of the classroom and brought them to the library to teach them how to play chess. He never brought any girls out of the classroom, which back in the seventies did not seem like an unusual practice.

And it wasn't the smartest boys in the class—like Frank—he took an interest in teaching the game of chess. It was those at the bottom of the academic ladder. Boys who needed to work on their math skills and who could benefit by learning the game and the critical thinking skills that it might develop. Boys like, say for instance, Giuseppe Basi.

It happened one Friday night in 1976 and still Frank did not learn about it until fifteen years later when Chef proposed to Babe, chose Frank to be his best man, and started World War III between the families when he refused to be married in the Catholic Church.

Frank pried the incident out of him at the rehearsal dinner prior to his wedding to Babe when he pleaded with him to reconsider his decision not to have the ceremony in the Church.

Chef Joe Bass was not drunk; not even a drop of alcohol had reached his lips. He was completely thoughtful and articulate, stone-sober in fact, and began by saying that what had happened to him, had happened to others but he knew that it did not happen to Frank and for this he was utterly grateful because he loved Frank like a brother and did not think he would have handled it well.

Frank sat in mournful silence while listening to Chef tell his story. There was not much more to be said other than the fact that Father Judd invited boys—the chess team—to the rectory every so often on Friday nights and on those nights the good priest smelled very similar to a homeless man when he took off all of his clothes.

You remember the smell of an unwashed human body, Chef had recounted to Frank, you can never forget it.

It happened twice before Chef Joe Bass physically attacked and pummeled Father Judd in the hallways of their Catholic grammar school from which he was expelled and forced to matriculate—along with other members of the chess team—into the vocational trade schools in the city of Niagara Falls.

"Do we know where the meeting is at?" Ambassador Melvin Reed asked Hairston Milbrand, III.

"We're waiting for confirmation from Ambassador Ortiz for the exact location," Milbrand, responded, "but it is probably at the Governorate."

"Ortiz? Why is he involved?"

"He is the Ambassador to the Holy See. It's not like we can sneak in the back door and not be noticed. Not with this parade in front of us."

"Alright, but I want him out of the room when we have Ratzinger."

"We may not have Ratzinger."

Ambassador Reed shot Frank a sideways glance. "Excuse me, we better have Ratzinger. I want that confirmed; now."

Milbrand hit his Blackberry. Frank remained silent while Reed took a call on his Blackberry from his daughter, a student at the nearby American University of Rome.

"We'll have dinner tonight at little later. Hold on just a second. Harry, do we have confirmation yet?"

"Well, Ratzinger is in the building and he may be there if his schedule permits. But he won't speak and he won't answer any questions."

"Excellent. Who else?"

"St. Onge, Sullivan, and Pietroangelo."

Reed looked at Frank for a sign-off on the list.

"Tell them we expect Cardinal Craxi. That was part of the request," Frank said.

Reed spoke into his cell phone.

"Gotta go, Julia. See you tonight." Reed put his phone away. "Do we have Craxi?"

A few moments passed while Milbrand worked his Blackberry.

"Yes we do. For ten minutes. We're meeting on the second floor."

"Ten minutes is plenty," Frank said.

"I understand you are not a very well-received man at the Governorate," Reed turned the conversation in the direction of Frank. "I heard about your incident with Ray Flynn in '96."

"Colorful guy," Frank responded.

"He's exactly why there should never be a Catholic appointed to the position I now hold; Flynn wrote the case study on it."

"Really."

"Yes, too emotional; too much conflict to bear for a regular church-going American Catholic to handle. The Italians wrote the book on the separation of Church and state, and sometimes for true believers that's just such a bitter pill to swallow."

"What about a non-Jewish Ambassador to Israel?"

"What about it? Happens all the time. Besides, it's an irrelevant position anyways."

"How's Silvio these days?," Frank could not resist the segue.

What did he care? He was nearly out of the business

completely. Finished. This trip to Rome was a throw-in from the boys and girls at Langley—a bon voyage gift for a solid but unspectacular career of singles, doubles, and one or two triples.

But no Home Runs.

Home Runs were the stuff of legends—of spooks—and Frank was certainly not a spook.

Frank had unearthed the matter at hand but it wasn't that big a deal. It would only become a big deal if the press got a hold of it and then it might become a very big deal.

Everyone in the Agency knew Frank had a Cialis-like hard-on for the Roman Catholic Church and that there was no better agent in the operations field when making a point in front of men dressed in red and white vestments. The Missionary Sisters of the Sacred Heart of Jesus—a female religious order that was openly hostile to the priesthood—had taught Frank well: *Speak up to Father. Look him straight in the eye. He is just a man. A servant of God, like you.*

"My friend Mr. Berlusconi appears to have had his pants sewn back on by his wife," Reed said.

"Yes but for how long?"

"In Italian politics, a year is a century. Who knows how long he may rule. He has less time than I would suppose that he imagines. And the Prime Minister has a very active imagination."

"How long might you have, Mr. Ambassador?"

"I'm afraid I don't understand your question, Mr. Bruno."

"Italy is ready to go nuclear. They voted to install reactors in power plants for the first time since 1987."

"A long overdue capitulation, wouldn't you say? We should be doing the same thing at home in the United States. Prime Minister Berlusconi is very forward-thinking man."

"The French must be laughing their asses off."

"How so?"

"They've been at it since the sixties. Now the Italians want to move forward. It's like Mussolini in the Savoy. It's a brilliant move by the Berlusconi administration. It keeps the heat off their debt situation; forces Areva to do business with them. The only other company that manufactures nuclear reactor technologies of any reliable value is Sendarro, the one you resigned from the Board of Directors of before accepting your ambassadorship."

"Look, we've arrived," Reed, said. "It's your show, Mr. Bruno."

The meeting occurred in a nondescript conference room on the second floor of the Palace of the Governorate, in a room bereft of any signposts of antiquity and utterly modern in its functional architecture. It could have been a conference room in an office park in America except that the walls were soundproof, there were no windows, and the men who were in attendance had not embraced the notion of casual Fridays.

They were in full black vestments, not the striking red and white gear befitting their stature as cardinals of the Church. *They* being Cardinal Valerie St. Onge (Secretariat of State), Frederick Sullivan (Prefect of the Apostolic Signatura) and Giancarlo Pietroangelo (Dean of Roman Rota).

"Will Cardinal Craxi be joining us?" Frank addressed the distinguished assembly of cardinals and their staff members seated at the conference table. Ambassador Reed took a seat in the corner of the room, as did Hairston Milbrand, III.

"He shall," replied Cardinal Umberto Craxi (Director of the Order of Religious Works), appearing in the doorway and occupying a seat next to Cardinal St. Onge. He was in his mid-fifties, extremely fit, and moved with the self-imposed discipline of a CEO.

"Thank you, gentlemen. May I start?" Frank did not have prepared notes to reference. He did not need them since only he and Cardinal Craxi would understand what he was about to say.

"The United States believes that the Church should begin to slowly and methodically unwind its positions in its Goldman Sachs Commodity Index funds, or as they are now known, the S&P GSI. These positions, held by various entities controlled by the Church, have realized an enormous profit. Quite simply it's time for you to step away."

"Mr. Bruno, may I be as blunt as you are?" Cardinal Craxi spoke up. "We were informed by Ambassador Reed that this was a matter of national security for the

United States. This appears to be a granular matter of finance. I do not see why his Holy Father has been asked to be present. Surely, you fail to grasp the arrogance of this request."

"As you can imagine," Frank continued, "Goldman Sachs has come under intense scrutiny during the past few years with the global financial crisis—their pivotal role in it—and, of course, their business practices which include the indexing of commodities.

"The contango wheat market is of particular concern to us as we wish to avoid another happenstance like the one in 2007 and 2008. That was when the price of wheat quadrupled in very short order and a global food crisis that should never have happened did so. We are just now understanding how Goldman Sachs and its close trading partners figured out how to game the commodities market."

"That theory has been disproved, Mr. Bruno. You may have read the *Economist* of June 2010."

"Thank you, Cardinal Craxi. We authored that article. It was in response to Frederick Kaufman's piece in Harper's that gave rise to many voices of alarm in markets. Big institutional money pouring into the purchasing of food commodities is a recent occurrence. Speculation in these markets used to be strictly limited. It's one thing for an investor to try to corner the gold market or take down a nation's currency à la George Soros.

"But food?

"No, that is not supposed to happen. The commodity markets for food were designed for producers to hedge. They were not intended for speculators to take control of the system and squeeze. But Goldman Sachs figured a way around this, and with its trading partners has completely upset, shall we say, the apple cart."

At that moment, a diminutive figure appeared in the conference room from a doorway Frank had not initially noticed. The only famous person to appear that much shorter in real life to him—other than the now present Joseph Alois Ratzinger, a.k.a the Holy Father, a.k.a Benedict XVI a.k.a Il Papa—was Prince Rogers Nelson, a.k.a the unpronounceable symbol.

In 1988, Frank and Chef took a cross-country trip in a rented Honda Accord and pulled into the parking lot of Tower Records on Sunset Boulevard in the Hollywood Hills to see what it was all about. Frank had just graduated from the Culinary Institute of America and had a summer to kill before he went to work for the federal government as a food service specialist, not an analyst, but as an actual chef from the CIA for the CIA. A black limousine pulled up alongside their Honda Accord and out popped the purple pants-wearing, pompadour-styling, pompous little troubadour from Minneapolis, Minnesota.

"Oh, my God, you're tiny!" exclaimed an incredulous Chef Joe Bass. "Dude, I really like the *Ballad of Dorothy Parker."*

That was how Frank felt now in the presence of Pope Benedict XVI who was flanked by several assistants, and who took a quiet seat at the head of the conference table. Ambassador Reed rushed to greet him but was waved off by the Pope's assistant secretary.

"Mr. Bruno, again," Cardinal Craxi spoke. "Thank you for your explanation of Anglo-Saxon finance but may I suggest that we reconvene this meeting at an appropriate time and place with my colleagues that does not infringe on the obligations of the Holy Father. This is something of which you have no understanding and cannot possibly conceive."

"Cardinal Craxi, may your brother Benedetto continue to rot in hell for refusing to extradite Abu Abbas and the rest of the hijackers of the Achille Lauro," Frank continued in his over-the-top, extra-crispy, dry delivery. "My entire career in government service has been about food. I was essentially a glorified cook before given the opportunity to go back to college, earn my degree, and then serve my country, which I have done for the past two decades.

"A cook, no less! It's true. For two years I was a chef before I entered a program to be in the intelligence service.

"Really, I have lived the American dream. Many of my colleagues chase far more glamorous things than I do—enriched uranium, weapons of mass destruction, high tech contraband, criminals, spies, money launders, terrorists.

"I am a food detective.

"I chase food all over the globe. Those that produce it and those that consume it. In the developing world, forty to sixty percent of a family's income is spent on feeding itself. If prices rise ten to twenty percent in a very short time then they go from two meals a day to one. That's when wars start and bombs are strapped to the backs of eighteen-year-olds to explode in public.

"One of the foods that has always fascinated me is wheat. The Church has known for centuries that wheat is what stabilizes populations. You are also the single largest mover of the wheat market."

"If only this were only so, Mr. Bruno," Cardinal Frederic Sullivan laughed. "There are far fewer Americans receiving Holy Communion on Sundays than in the past. When was the last time you received the Holy Eucharist?"

"Yes, but not in Asia, Africa or South America where your flock continues to grow. You really can't create the demand for wheat and then profit from it on the futures market. It would be very unseemly to do so again. As to your direct question, Cardinal Sullivan, I am requesting the administration of the sacrament right now. That is why I am so profoundly grateful for the presence of the Holy Father at this moment."

It wasn't a bad way for Frank Bruno to go out; down on his knees, requesting communion from the Pope.

His petition was met by the keenly observant intellect of Benedict XVI, while a bewildered and befuddled Ambassador Reed and Charge d'affaires Milbrand observed the sudden and pagan turn of events in rapt silence.

Surely this was a bizarre request to non-Catholics, such as the Ambassador or the Charge d'affaires—the mere image of which was certain to spell closure to Frank Bruno's career with the CIA—but not to Frank or, for that matter, Joseph Alois Ratzinger.

After all, if they were to embrace the literal interpretation of the transmodal nature of the nattily dressed little fella with the red kippah, Frank's request was not all that misplaced or ill-timed, especially since there was a ciborium within reach of the conference table.

From the Pope's hands to Frank's tongue passed the unleavened wheat that came to represent the body and blood of Jesus Christ, a Jew from Nazareth, crucified by decree under Pontius Pilate. It had been ten years—perhaps even longer—since he had received the Host. His memory was peculiarly faulty on this matter. For the past twenty years, it had crawled incessantly, like a spider indexing web code for any points of interests or divergence in his general environment, but on this question—the matter of sacraments—it was registering a common error code.

```
Error 404: Not found
```

Frank made the sign of the cross in one of his last acts as an employee of the CIA. The final gesture was another request of the Pope, a reverse order of things, as Frank knew them to be, but essential to his orderly transition to civilian life.

"Will you now please grant my confession?"

Four

Frank remained in Rome for a few days longer at the Hotel Londra next to Piazza Sallustio, hanging out and playing cards with the locals in a bar hidden inside the gated Piazza where there was a collection of government offices in which no one took their jobs very seriously. They all took the presence of this hidden bar seriously; mobbing it in the morning for cappuccino and cornetti, back at ten from their desks for another espresso, back at three for another, back at six for the commute home and then the Piazza's local residents streamed in around nine for cards, whiskey, and gossip.

He ate his meals at Cantina Cantarini across the street like so many others, spellbound by the authenticity of this family-run *trattoria* whose Roman formality and manners were extended by the family that ran it. It made him feel like he was at home in Niagara Falls at Restaurant Giuseppe Basi, with Babe coming over to his table to chit-chat while people he had known for decades stopped by his table to ask him how many people he had killed lately.

"How's things with the government, Frankie; still chasing the terrorists?"

Frank felt as if he would be content to remain within the radius of Piazza Sallustio for his entire life if only he could devise a way to make money—a boatload of it—from this droopy oasis. The alarm bell had sounded for Frank nearly a year ago. He was forty then, unmarried, no children, and his mother Ramona had all but given up hope that he would settle down.

He needed to make money.

You don't just walk away from a twenty-year career with the CIA. You run away from it to make money, unless of course you come to the decision to make money while in the employ of the CIA, and that was never an option for Frank Bruno.

He would never make Melvin P. Reed type-money—brokered, borrowed, stolen, and leveraged—nor Hairston Milbrand III money—inherited, compounded, receding and squandered—but he wanted to make enough money so that he might return to a place like this in his later years with a flock of near-grown children and a reformed ex-Faustian wife to again play cards in the solitude of these palm trees, in the city he loved most next to his native city of Niagara Falls, while drinking some wine at Cantina Cantarini.

It would still be here, he thought. Places like this, and Restaurant Giuseppe Basi, never closed.

The ringtone on his cell phone—"Mount Airy Groove" by Pieces of Dream—interrupted his meditative contemplation of the next phase of his life. He hadn't even touched the plate of penne all'arrabbiata set in front of him a half an hour ago. He flipped open his phone to retrieve the text message and recoiled.

"Call me. Something has happened to Joe."

Frank immediately found Babe La Bruna's number stored in his phone and placed the call, which rolled over to voicemail. He called his mother, a non-cell phone adherent, and that call went unanswered as well. He tried Babe again with the same result. The best he could do was head back to the Hotel and hope by then that somebody would respond.

The thing that kept turning in Frank's mind was that nothing ever happened to Joe Bass unless Joe Bass had initiated it. He was imperturbable. He had always known his destiny from early days and it was to cook food for others.

"Call me. Something has happened to Joe."

Something could only mean that something *bad* had happened to Chef Joe Bass.

Finally, Frank reached his mother Ramona on the fourth attempt. She was sobbing hysterically. She said that Joe had been murdered; that he had been stabbed in the kitchen of his restaurant. The police were investigating. She could not reach Babe. She had been called by Cousin Leonard who—God bless his simple soul—was all types of confused.

Ramona Bruno asked her son to come home immediately. She cried some more when she mentioned a tale as familiar to Frank as the biblical depiction of Moses's adoption. Giuseppe was the name given to this infant boy awarded by the State to the Basi family who lived in the cottage house behind theirs. This little boy—a mere six pounds with dazzling hazel eyes—was unusually quiet and thoughtful but what joy he had brought into all of their lives. What joy he brought to the millions who knew him as Chef Joe Bass. They had watched this boy grow into a man and do great things, achieve far beyond the abandoned moment of his birth; and he had now been left on the floor of a restaurant kitchen, like an animal, to bleed to death.

All five families of red sauce royalty from the local restaurant community attended the funeral services for Chef Joe Bass that did not include, by codicil of last will and testament, a Mass of Christian Burial.

There was Alfredo Cuneo of *Da Alfredo,* Norman Panepinto of *Stormin' Norman's House of Sauce,* Nelson Tabone of *Neddy's House of Spaghetti,* Pietro Prato of *A Mano,* and finally, dressed in an expensive three-piece custom tailored suit, Bebe Lo Piccolo of *Piccolo Mondo.*

Frank made it in time as well; a late night flight out of Fiumicino to Lester B. Pearson International Airport in Toronto, landing him with just enough time to grab a rental car and scamper down the Queen Elizabeth

Expressway to the Rainbow Bridge in Niagara Falls, and from there to the M.J. Colucci funeral home on 19th Street near Ferry Avenue.

Babe received him with her hand covering her mouth, as close to a state of dishevelment as Frank had ever seen her in, with a giant set of sunglasses hiding her swollen eyes.

"In his kitchen, Frank," Babe La Bruna sobbed. "In his kitchen!"

Frank took Babe's arm and escorted her into a private room. They embraced in the frantic manner grief-stricken people do when they have no idea what to say to each other.

"Have the police told you anything?" Frank finally spoke.

"Not much. They talked to me for most of yesterday and again this morning."

"Who found him?"

"Leonard. I had been with him that morning. It was a crazy morning. He opened the door to the restaurant and somebody had left a burner on the stove with an extinguished pilot. He thought it might have been deliberate but that's just Joe with his wild imagination. It was probably whoever closed, knocking the valve on with the back of the mop or something. Joe smelled gas, went to investigate, and tripped and hit his head."

"I thought he was stabbed?"

"He was stabbed. This happened before he was stabbed. I'm telling you it was a crazy, crazy morning."

"Do the police know this?"

"Of course they know this. Leonard found him lying on the floor of the restaurant. He probably had a mild concussion. They opened the kitchen door and the smell of the gas nearly knocked them both over. He opened the back door to vent the place."

"Did he call the cops?"

"My husband, call the cops. That'd be the day. No, he did what he always did, which was to continue to do his work. When I came in to do the deposit, we talked for a while. I can't remember if we argued about something or what we said. The only thing I remember was his eyes were sort of glassy. He looked a little wobbly."

"How did you find out?"

"I was at the bank. I thought Joe was calling me to pick something up for him. When I answered, I heard Leonard."

"I'm so sorry Babe. I can't believe this is happening."

"There was so much blood on his chef's coat, Frank. It was soaked red straight through. You wouldn't have believed it."

"Did they find the knife?"

"They found six knives. All restaurant cutlery. You know what a freak Joe was about his cutlery. We have a sharpener in here twice a week. They had all been run through the dishwasher."

Outside the funeral home, television satellite uplink trucks lined the street, and the police cordoned off a buffer zone for the press and the curiosity seekers. Chef Joe Bass's homicide was a very big deal in this town. He had achieved the rank of national celebrity by means other than crime and politics (in this municipality these were two sides of the same coin) or by going over the Falls in a steel contraption, and, despite his recent setbacks, he was still a much-beloved and larger-than-life figure.

The Food Network ran a hastily edited one-hour special on the life and times of Chef Joe Bass (1967–2010) that aired the following evening. Various celebrity chefs, none of whom could stand nor comprehend his meteoric success and downfall, appeared in glowing testimonials about the rugged sensibility of a Chef who championed the poor man's pantry of Italian-American favorites. Chef Joe Bass was not afraid to tell Susie Homemaker or the Culinary Elite from the set of his television show that what they were serving was a Disaster Area.

Mario Batali registered the most carefully calibrated tribute to Chef when referring to him, not as a Chef in the classical sense, but a *'Mezzo Cuoco'*—a half cook who knew just enough about everything in the kitchen—and who had crafted a distinct set of gastronomic norms that would someday find their way onto the back labels of every jar of canned tomato sauce in America.

Cousin Leonard inadvertently paid Chef more

damning praise when, overcome by grief, he delivered an impromptu eulogy at the wake that began with the following inauspicious opening statement: "Joe always paid me in cash…on the count of my accident…"

Frank had little time to step back and digest the scene before him. A return to his native city had always required a period of suspended disbelief and chemical reorganization within his brain, similar to that of scuba diver seeking to avoid the bends. Nothing ever changed here but things always remained a little worse; a little larger than life in a heroic sense but tattered and inoperable in the physical.

Chef's first grade teacher came to pay her respects; so did Chef's truant officer. Chef's swarm of ex- and present girlfriends came by with an implied sense of grief and loss equal to that of Babe La Bruna, who, to her credit, refused to acknowledge their putana-like gaudiness, and sent them Cousin Leonard's way to be shown the back door. Politicians came by to be seen and photographed. And of course everyone and anyone in the restaurant business came as well.

You were either in Chef Joe Bass's camp in this regard or you were against him. It was blue versus gray. Chef's disciples in the business of food wore gray. You either understood how he rose from obscurity, serving essentially the same menu as thousands of other ill-financed, family-run enterprises in the crowded Italian-American family dining category, or you thought everything that Chef Joe Bass cranked out of his kitchen was overrated.

You either seethed jealousy that this man should have been plucked from his kitchen, put on national television, and be allowed to tell credentialed Chefs, food opinion makers, prophets of vegetarianism, locavorism, and whatever else was currently trendy in food business, to go fuck themselves; or you rooted for him by mobbing his personal appearances and buying the merchandise he sold from his website.

You probably favorited the video clip of him on You Tube at the Aspen Food Classic—the annual gathering of culinary titans, food press, and luminaries—when he delivered his now famous remarks that polarized the entire food industry in the way Oliver Stone's Gordon Gecko energized an entire generation of Wall Street neubians—'A Happy Meal is not a Disaster Area…A Happy Meal is Pure Genius.'

Based on that statement alone, Chef was awarded his first corporate endorsement by Kraft Foods, and laughed all the way to the bank with the check that had been issued him to kick-start his deal. It was for an amount so grossly inflated and untethered to any actual work that he had to perform—not a potato peeled, not a pot set to water—that only then did he realize that he had tapped into to the great corporate inferiority complex of food executives who want to be taken seriously at things such as the Aspen Food Classic.

But for others, like Bebe Lo Piccolo, the funeral of Chef Joe Bass was personal.

Lo Piccolo came as one of the big swinging dicks of red sauce royalty in the restaurant industry. His

Piccolo Mondo out-grossed Restaurant Giuseppe Basi four-fold. Lo Piccolo did more covers with his Early Bird special on a Tuesday than Chef Joe Bass did in an entire weekend. He served shit on a plate, made a fortune in the process, but could not so much as register an acknowledgment from Chef Joe Bass, not even a localized designation of his seventeen thousand five hundred square foot monstrosity as an official Disaster Area.

Bebe Lo Piccolo attended the funeral with a purpose—to make sure Chef Joe Bass was indeed dead in the casket—and to fire a spit ball from the hollowed tip of his Bic pen straight into Chef's unibrow so that it would stick to the caked-on makeup that had been applied to his skin.

He also came to present Babe La Bruna with an envelope.

"Hello, Frank," Bebe Lo Piccolo said.

"Bebe," Frank nodded his head, more of an acknowledgement of the offensive sting from Lo Piccolo's after shave—*Rockford* by Atkinson—a defunct Euro-scent traded on the Internet by cologne geeks.

"I'm sorry for your loss. Is Babe here?"

"Yes. She's just stepped out for moment to compose herself."

"This is shocking."

"To say the least."

"Any idea what happened?"

"I just got here myself. I have no idea."

"That's right. I forgot. You're one of those spooks. I

heard some stories about you. Joe liked to brag about his cousin—the big spy."

"Anything he told you in that regard was highly overstated. I was a commodities analyst for the government."

"A what? To tell you the truth, Frank, I always thought you were finocchio."

"Thanks Bebe. That is very funny."

"You never did get married. No kids. You used to hang around with that artsy crowd, the chicks who used to take their tops off, throw paint on their titties and then launch themselves against the walls. That's what they called art. You went to the Culinary Institute. Now, I remember."

"That was a long time ago."

"Why didn't you ever get into the business?"

"I kinda did for a while, sideways. I had other interests. How's business?"

"Business is great. Fabulous. We're putting on another banquet room for four hundred. We've got the Canadians coming down from Toronto on the weekends. They do a three-hour shopping spree at the outlet mall and then they are bussed over to the restaurant. The Canadian dollar is at par with the U.S. dollar. They're like pigs in shit, those fucking Norks. The Canadian guys come down here with their wives, to drink their Canadian beer for a buck a bottle cheaper than what they pay up in Canada, watch football on the television, and get drunk. The Canadian women want to come down here, shop for a while, let their husbands get drunk, and get laid. I get a blow job every Friday and Saturday night by a housewife from Mississauga."

"Sounds like you have life all figured out."

"Your cousin was a lousy prick. That building where his restaurant stands should have been mine. My father worked for the Old Man back in the day. That's my history there."

"Joe took a gamble. It was for sale for almost twenty years."

"Listen, I came here to give Babe this envelope. I want to do the right thing. Your cousin pissed a lot of people off around here, running around in that Camaro like it was 1982 or something. He pissed people off up in Buffalo. He owes me money."

"Bebe, can you please step off for just a second?"

"OK, finocchio," Lo Piccolo's nostrils flared. "I just want to do the right thing here. Swear to Christ I wish they hadn't cremated him. I wanted to spit in his face but that would be bad for business. So let's end our little chat here. You give Babe this envelope and I'll give you two weeks for a reply."

"Let me kick you in the ass on the way out."

Whatever re-orientation or reprogramming was required for him to get back in the proper mindset had now vanished. Frank was back in Niagara Falls and it felt good.

FIVE

For the first time since the start of its operating history, Restaurant Giuseppe Basi sat closed for more than two consecutive days. Chef Joe Bass's ashes were potted in a nondescript urn provided by the crematorium. Entombment in a marble-faced, milk box-sized slot in St. Joseph's mausoleum would have been another clear violation of Chef's last wishes. So he was shelved next to a selection of twelve-year-old Scotch at the restaurant's bar, not because he had expressly requested this, but because that's where there was room for the urn.

It was the first hopeful sign that Babe was seriously considering re-opening the place, or at least that's how Cousin Leonard, Bobo, Jason, and Pops interpreted it, along with the service staff who had gallantly volunteered, without pay, to do a deep-cleanse of the restaurant the week after Chef's murder.

Cousin Leonard personally handled the spot where he found Chef's body. He bleached it multiple times but continued to find tiny blood spots splattered into the nooks and crevices of the surrounding kitchen equipment.

Frank visited Babe at the restaurant every day. She sat in her office staring out the window or curled up on the couch—texting, texting, texting—to whom Frank had neither the heart nor the curiosity to inquire. Finally, he confronted her when she would not respond to his most basic entreaties.

"Babe, you are going to have to tell the staff something. A restaurant is not something that can just sit idle."

"You're right. I do have to speak to them. People have to work and feed their families. I would have never thought this restaurant could survive without Joe. He owned every bit of it. He could put his finger on everything in here. If a complaint came in, he jumped on it. From just a few simple words out of customer's mouth he could deduce what went wrong, and more than often it was a service issue. If it was the food, forget it. He would be intolerable."

"I've been hanging onto something since the funeral," Frank said. "Bebe Lo Piccolo gave it to me the night of the wake. He says to open it and give him an answer. Do you want to look at it now?"

"What is it?"

"An envelope."

"He wants an answer. That's what he said. I'm supposed to provide an answer to that dirt bag."

"I can toss it."

"No, let's look at it. Let's have a laugh."

Babe opened the letter at her desk. A certified bank check in the amount of $450,000 fluttered out from the tri-fold of the cover letter. It was an official purchase offer for the property, contents, and naming rights to Restaurant Giuseppe Basi.

Real estate values in the City of Niagara Falls, New York had remained historically depressed since the near-complete disintegration of the local electrochemical industry during the seventies. Joe Bass originally paid twenty-five thousand dollars for the building that included a twenty-spot parking lot. Today, the restaurant grossed an impressive two million in sales (reported income remained a tad under 1.5 million), but it was the good will of the restaurant's name—Giuseppe Basi—that carried the bulk of the transaction's projected value.

How do you valuate a namesake restaurant after the namesake of said restaurant has been murdered in cold blood?

Some would argue that this now infamous incident had increased the value of the restaurant (in a Spark's-Steakhouse-meets-Paul Castellano sort of way). Others might be inclined to run the other way, making the case that the restaurant could never recover from such a fatal blow to the linchpin of its success, especially a restaurant that bore such an indelible name as Restaurant Giuseppe Basi.

"Well now, I wasn't expecting that," said Babe.

"What was your expectation?"

"I don't know. Lo Piccolo is such a child. I thought maybe he was going to propose to me or something bizarre, now that I'm a widow."

"Maybe you should take another look at it."

"For what? It's inconceivable that I would sell him this place. He knows that."

"Babe, you're forty-two years old. Do you really want to be on your feet all night waiting to close a restaurant?"

"What else would I do? This is all I've done for the last decade and a half. I've lived and breathed this place every waking moment of my life."

"That's why I think you should sit down and let's discuss this. Forget about the offer. Forget about the number. This is about you. Do you really want to stay here without Joe?"

"We talked about it, you know. We used to tease each other—like all couples in this business do—about what would happen if one of us suddenly wasn't here."

"And?"

"And we said we'd deal with it however you deal with something like that. But we'd open up for business as usual and carry on."

"You really think you can carry on here, knowing what happened to Joe?"

"Joe's been gone from this place for a long time. We've been apart in every way except for the legal declaration. He hadn't worked a night here in God-knows how long. He was off in New York, or running around with his toys and his girlfriends. He was not a man of subtlety, Frank. Yes, this was his vision, his food. But I carried this place."

"I know you have, Babe. But maybe it's time to walk away."

"No you don't, Frank. I found myself out on that floor, night after night. I enjoyed it. You see the key to a restaurant's success is not the food. It's the service. I treated everyone the same way—respect. Every low-life to every high-brow that walked through those doors. Because when it comes to food and service, the most serious mistake you can make in this business is to underestimate an individual's ability to taste. Joe thought almost everyone was a moron when it came to food but I never did."

"You're exhausted; I can see it in your eyes. Any news from the police?"

"No; not really. They interviewed me again. They don't have anything other than the fact that Joe left the kitchen door open, which of course was unusual in January but when you consider what happened that morning, with the gas and all..."

"Who's the detective?"

"Here," Babe said, handing him the card of Detective Nathan Sensabaugh. "He says they have print marks from the snow to boots that don't match anyone here at the restaurant. They don't have a vehicle or an eyewitness."

"I'll call him this afternoon. See what's up."

"What about you? What's up with you?"

"I have to go to D.C. tomorrow and clean up some loose ends."

"You're really walking away from everything?"

"I've thought about it for long time. I have some things I want to do; some opportunities to explore."

"What do you do, anyway? Turn in some secret badge or something like that? Somebody zaps your brain and you forget the secret handshake?"

"More or less."

Babe had moved to the couch and stretched out her legs. Her black hair angled over her cheekbones like a curtain to be brushed back in a moment of revelatory beauty. She maintained the physique of a woman half her age. Frank could not remember a time when he was not affected, in some way or another, by her presence.

"I was kind of hoping you might stick around a little," she said. "Help me get through this, just for a little while longer."

"Me? What could I do?"

"I'd make you a prep cook."

"Perfect. That would make my life complete. Back here in the Falls, living amongst the people. Can I work days and get paid cash? I don't want to screw up my unemployment check. You know I get one of those; just like Leonard."

"We'll have to negotiate," Babe laughed deeply for the first time. "I want you to hear this," she said and put her cell phone on speaker. "Yes, Bebe Lo Piccolo please...Babe La Bruna."

Bebe Lo Piccolo came on the line after a short hold. His voice was a study in strained formality.

"Hello, Babe. How are you doing with everything?"

"Bebe, I have you on speaker. Frank is here with me. He gave me your envelope."

"Hello, Frank."

"Greetings," Frank said, not knowing where any of this was going, but enjoying the spectacle. Frank had sat in on conversations that he could never reveal—exchanges between presidents, generals and senators—and this conversation carried the same crackle of charged human electricity.

"So you want to buy my restaurant. This is very flattering, Bebe. Why would you even bother with such a small operation like ours? We don't even have a private room for parties. It's too small for what you do."

"I've always admired what you did with the space, Babe. What you and Joe did, I should say. It's a beautiful space. It has a special place in history. It's a legacy I want to be sure, you know, survives."

"So how did you come up with this number? And why send me a certified check without having the decency to ask me first if I was interested in selling?"

"Ah," Lo Piccolo laughed nervously. "That's a little trick I learned from a real estate agent. If I'm really serious about a property, I always send my final offer first in the form of a certified check. You and I know Niagara Falls is a shithole. That property isn't worth anything without the name Giuseppe Basi on the front door. But forget about the number for a second. Let's talk about the thought of you selling to me. Is that something, you know, that interests you?"

Babe did not answer. She let the line go silent until Lo Piccolo spoke up again.

"Babe, are you there?"

"I'm here. I'm just pondering all the ways you could serve your shoe leather if you got your hands on this place."

"Oh, that's brilliant. I thought we were having an adult conversation."

"Of course you could blow out one of the walls and put a souvenir shop up in the front. The tourists would have to walk by it twice on their way out the door. Are you giving away sherbet with the chicken picatta or are you upgrading them to the Golfo di Sorrento package with the tiramisu at the end of the meal?"

"You're in way over your head, Babe. I could hire your entire kitchen staff, double their salaries in a heartbeat, and then where would you be?"

"I'd be clawing on my knees back to you. Begging you to serve that shoe leather."

"Cunt."

Frank made his decision right then. He was going to stick around for a few months when he got back from D.C. He wanted to be sure Babe hadn't become completely unhinged and driven herself off a cliff. He did not need the next words she said in response to Bebe Lo Piccolo to solidify his thoughts, yet nevertheless they crystallized what Graham Allison had wrote long ago as the essence of decision making. When Frank first read that textbook in preparation for his entry into the CIA; the notions of decision making were thought to be organizational rather than biological. But from where he sat now, observing Babe, he realized that truly local decision making in Niagara Falls, New York came from the gospel according to Saint Mario (as in Puzo).

"You can have my answer now, Lo Piccolo. My answer is no. And I would appreciate it if you kept yourself, and all of your scummy crew, out of my restaurant."

When one restaurateur bans another from their premises, it is, as they say, ON.

Babe's chin dropped down to her chest. She stood up, brushed her hair back, and walked over to her desk. She grabbed another business card from a stack of papers and handed it to Frank.

"Could you at least call this bitch for me? She's hounded me since last week. She wants to come and do a story on what's next for the restaurant. On what happened to Joe. I don't want to deal with her now. But if I'm going to reopen, I need to spin a yarn, and she has the juice nationally to do us some good."

The card contained a Manhattan cell prefix, no office address, logo, or corporate affiliation. It belonged to the most powerful voice in the food blogosphere. Her voice had arisen from a sporadic appearance as a short feature contributor to the *New York Times* in the Food section, followed by some savage reviews as a fill-in restaurant critic.

Her take-down of exalted chefs in the celebrity culinary world was the stuff of legend; and since most every chef that encountered her—male and female alike—wanted to please and impress her in more than a gastronomic manner of speaking, she was granted access to kitchen and culinary secrets that were previously the domain of only those inside, higher up in the trade.

This gave her writing credibility. She devoured her subjects. She never made the mistake of confusing food with politics or religion. If anything, her writing was highly sexual, descriptive, erotic. She didn't start out to become the Anaïs Nin of the culinary universe but after strapping on a chef or two; allowing herself to be bent over a prep table (a common male culinary fantasy) to get to where she needed to go in the story, she was not about to change her approach.

It worked.

And after reading any one of her riveting entries, one came away without snickering at the title of her blog—*The Buck Stopped Here*—thinking it perfectly plausible that she had consumed the entire contents of each subject matter, protein, fats, carbohydrates, and entrails all.

"Who in the hell is Hayden Buckingham?" Frank wondered with a sense of professional unease before he dialed her number and waited for a response.

Six

They met at Vietnam Georgetown Restaurant on 30th and M Streets for dinner to discuss how Hayden Buckingham might write the *Life and Death of Chef Joe Bass* for a cover feature in the *Sunday New York Times*. Buckingham jumped at the opportunity for the meeting, catching a shuttle from New York to D.C. the very day Frank had called her and left a message. Before he could reply to the message she left on his cell, Hayden Buckingham was already in D.C. and texting him for directions to their meet-up.

Frank had chosen the location out of sentimentality.

It was the place, back in 1984, where he first experienced a type of Asian food other than Chinese. Vietnam Georgetown was established in 1973 and it was the first Vietnamese restaurant in the nation's capital. When Frank was at culinary school, Asian food was not part of the curriculum, as it was now, and his wildly tangential (or was it manifest destiny?) entry into the intelligence service had opened his mind to the possibility that despite his degree and training, he knew very little about food at all.

The facade to Vietnam Georgetown appeared the same to Frank as he remembered it back in 1984. The interior seemed to have the same sparse decor but it was clean and comforting by way of its unadorned longevity. In the most transient of all American cities, the fact that Vietnam Georgetown remained unscathed, in the same family hands, and at the same location—borne of a terrible, brutal, and senseless war whose veterans were now old and grey—was a feat that genuinely endeared it to him. The food and service here were nothing extraordinary to modern expectations of Southeast Asian cuisine. Again, it was the backstory and the location of the restaurant that kept people coming here, year after year, and the fact that they were always open when others were closed.

Vietnam had no longer signified war in the American consciousness. More often, it meant spring rolls, báhn mì, and lemongrass. Restaurants are the appropriate and final response when military conflict proves unsustainable

At least that's what his father, Dominick Bruno, a Vietnam veteran who first introduced him to the restaurant, had said to Frank while he was an active duty Army colonel stationed at the Pentagon. Frank wanted to understand his father, or at least come close to grasping what he had experienced during the war, and these sporadic lunches at Vietnam Georgetown gave him the first prolonged period of conversation with his father about his war experiences.

Dominick Bruno had been estranged from the family from almost the moment he returned from the Philippines in 1975, after serving three tours in Vietnam as a Green Beret. Dominick Bruno was a professional soldier, not some bearded, drug-addicted cartoon of psychotic behavior that Frank saw depicted on television and at the movies while growing up. His father maintained an indestructible sense of self-discipline and personal honor.

As a teenager, Frank became incensed that the stories of professional career officers who came back after the Vietnam war and continued to serve in the military were never made a part of popular American culture. He would change that someday, he thought, but later abandoned the idea while searching for his own identity.

Frank sought approval from his father at one particular lunch at Vietnam Georgetown on his career choices. He knew very early in life that his path to manhood was inextricably bound to the process of becoming his father. His father knew this as well and did not object to Frank's decision to attempt to join the CIA.

Hayden Buckingham was even more punctual than Frank for their initial meeting. He had her blog image to reference but Buckingham had nothing to go on other than intuition as to what Frank looked like. She rose out of her seat the moment he entered the restaurant, extending her arm, and smiled an absurdly magnanimous grin. Frank remembered reading somewhere that women had a larger degree of muscle contraction while smiling than men; apparently it was an evolutionary response for survival.

"I am grateful for this meeting," Hayden Buckingham said.

"Yes, well, I hope I can help. Babe is determined to carry on with the business, and there is a concern as to how this might affect things."

"I understand completely. What I don't yet understand is what happened to Joe. This still seems all very shocking. Have the police made any arrests?"

"No. Not that I am aware of. I plan on returning there soon to help Babe out and get her feet back on the ground."

"Was it a robbery? I know the restaurant is in a transitional neighborhood."

"Hah, that's one way to describe it. The entire city of Niagara Falls is transitioning to third world status."

"That's something I didn't realize until I did my first piece on Joe. It's as bad as Newark or East St. Louis, isn't it?"

"It's worse. There are over eight million visitors every year and yet the city itself, outside of the periphery of the Falls, remains a blighted mess."

"Why is that?"

"When the manufacturing plants left, the taxable base that supported all the corruption and the graft dried up."

"And Joe bought a famous mobster's funeral home and turned it into a highly rated restaurant. There are hundreds of Italian restaurants in New York—some very famous with famous chefs and owners—and most of them try very hard to be authentic. But Joe's restaurant was the definition of authenticity. You had the feeling of being guided by one singular narrative from the kitchen, one precise story of the way things are supposed to be cooked."

"Joe was the best." Frank felt sucker-punched, acknowledging that the loss of his lifelong friend had still not fully exerted its sorrow over him.

"You weren't related to him?"

"No we were not related."

"He spoke about you. I know of your background."

"Shall we order something to drink?" Frank inquired. "Do you drink sake?"

"Not if I can drink wine. This is such an old-school restaurant. You don't come here for the food, do you?"

"No, you come here because they are almost always open, clean, and they were the first back in the seventies. It's the continuation of the war itself. Food is the only happy ending to a war. The location helps, also."

They ordered a Gigondas.

Hayden Buckingham maintained a formal set of dining manners, a calm sense of having wine poured out for her, and an attentive but not overbearing disposition to the recitation of the evening's specials. Her beyond shoulder-length, blond hair was tied in the back and slung in one long ponytail. She was tall, nearly six feet. She had blue-grey eyes that did not overwhelm. It was the gentle slope from her forehead to the tip of her slightly upturned nose that ensconced you in her beauty—the jumping off point to her lower lip that was demarcated by an ancient injury (perhaps a stitch or two to close a busted lip) right in the middle of her kisser.

Frank had a fascination for life's longest lasting physical scars. They never failed to intrigue him on how they were acquired.

"To Giuseppe Basi," he said. "An original."

"To Chef Joe Bass. Would he think this place is a Disaster Area?"

"He would be on his knees begging entrance to the kitchen. Joe was a restaurant historian. My father took us here when we were teenagers and visited him in D.C. Joe's mind was blown by the ingredients and the rice noodle soup. He said it was a revelation."

"Your father? I remember Joe saying something about your father."

"Yes, he was a career military officer," Frank caught himself in mid-sentence and mid-memory. Damn, this Hayden Buckingham was good at turning her subjects completely around. He rarely talked this much when meeting someone for the first time.

"So, the son followed in the father's footsteps in some way."

"Not quite. I was DQ'd from joining the army my senior year of high school. I suffered a knee injury playing football and that wrecked my scholarship to West Point."

"But why the move to the CIA?"

"The Culinary Institute?"

"Yes," Hayden Buckingham laughed, "I guess I should distinguish between the two."

"Well, I was young and impulsive. When it became clear that my injury had voided my appointment—my local congressman had already nominated me and I was accepted—I kind of freaked out. I wanted to work with my hands. Food was the single biggest thing in our family. Just look at Joe. He was not related to me by blood but ever since we were boys we ate almost all of our meals together. And he cooked many of them."

"Yes, I know this history. I wrote it."

"Going to the Culinary Institute was very different back then," Frank said. "All the instructors were old, stodgy German and French chefs from abroad. There was a sense of discipline, almost military in nature. It was like being at a military academy come to think of it. It was not a glamorous or sexy choice. What I really wanted to do was travel and I needed a skill set I could carry with me as my passport. That's why I joined the government. I figured if they didn't want me in the military, I could weasel my way into the field in some other way if I could just get stationed overseas."

"That's pretty ingenious of you. How old were you when you decided this?"

"Eighteen. I graduated from Culinary at twenty. I joined the government through the GSA, and in less than a year I was stationed at the American embassy in Moscow as a sous chef. Now, shall we turn our attention to the matter at hand?" Frank asked, refilling their glasses and ordering another bottle of Gigondas. "My concern about any more publicity is that it could cripple the restaurant."

"Impossible," Hayden stated with utter confidence. "Until now, Chef Joe Bass was merely famous. He had a huge following. The Food Network really didn't know what to do with him after the Larry King incident. He was always quite unpredictable. But his death turned him into legend."

"Yes, that is exactly my concern. I was hoping you might give the restaurant a chance to recover before you wrote anything about it. It will not be the same without Joe. It's going to take time to see whether it can survive."

"I'm not interested in the food or the service or even the colorful clientele at Restaurant Giuseppe Basi," Hayden said, between sips of the Gigondas. "Been there. Done that. No; I want to find out who killed him."

Seven

The first full prep shift in anticipation of the re-opening of Restaurant Giuseppe Basi began six weeks after Chef Joe Bass's murder. Cousin Leonard met Frank at the kitchen entrance to the restaurant at seven a.m. and keyed open the door. He had trouble disarming the newly installed alarm system. The security code had been written down for him on a slip of paper and hidden inside his wallet for just such an occasion. But Cousin Leonard had a terrible habit of putting his wallet and cigarettes out while drinking at bars, three sheets to the wind, and they had been swiped the night before.

Frank called Babe on his cell, explained the situation, and accessed the code to silence the piercing alarm.

"We're in," he said. "This should be quite the adventure. Cousin Leonard looks rather hung over."

"Welcome back to the restaurant business, Frank," Babe said. "I really appreciate your pitching in. Think of it as a working vacation. You're getting back to your roots."

Frank had another call waiting on his cell. He clicked over to the trembling voice of his mother, Ramona. The newspaper arrived at about this time every day and he assumed that she must have read the obituary section already and was informing him, as was her practice, of another distant relative's passing.

"Frank, there's a letter here from the Catholic Church."

"OK. Go ahead and open it."

"I already did. You're being excommunicated. It looks very official."

"Not now, Mom. It's probably just a form letter. I have to make chicken stock. I'll call you later."

"It's signed by a Cardinal Umberto Craxi. Frank, what have you done?"

"He's a criminal, Mom. He's been speculating on the wheat futures market for years, taking advantage of all the instability of commodities and the food supply. He's done so to the enormous profit of the Church and to Cardinal Craxi his damn self. Mom, the whole world food supply is a tinderbox. How much did you pay for zucchini this week?"

"I don't remember."

"OK. Milk, eggs, butter."

"Everything is so expensive these days."

"Exactly, Mom. The world is ready for a great inflationary run up because our governments keep printing money and piling up debt. The U.S. has been able to fill in the gaps in the world food supply in the past, creating a buffer or a safety net, but that's not so easy with all the money that's out there and the ability of global financial giants who can rig the markets and scoop up that money. Demand keeps rising. Supply is unstable. Think of all those countries like Venezuela who want "food sovereignty," and yet they can't even feed their own people because they artificially put price controls on basic food items. Now, multiply that one little dictator—that pudgy little Hugo Chavez (his basic issues are food- related, as is his type two diabetes (he's a carb addict)—by one hundred. That's the kind of shit I've been involved in for the past two decades and I needed a break."

"Frank, are you on drugs?"

"No, Mom. You asked me a question and I am answering it. Cardinal Craxi is a criminal and I called him on it. I did it in front of the Pope."

"The Pope? You didn't tell me you saw the Pope."

"Yes, Mom. He gave me communion. And he heard my confession."

"Confession. Oh, Frank, what have you done?"

"Not now. I have to make chicken stock. Did Grandma use bones or whole chickens to make her stock?"

"Whole chickens. Joe would have done the same. She would bring a pot of water to boil with the chickens in it. Then she would dump the water out and start again with the same chickens. It was her way of making sure the chickens were clean. That the liquid was clean."

"That's a Chinese method."

"Chinese? What are you talking about?"

"The Chinese make their stock like that, Mom."

"We never called it stock. That's a fancy name. We call it broth. Joe called it brodo when he went fancy."

"Stock. Broth. Joe never went fancy, Mom. Now I have to hang up and make broth."

Nothing else matters when there is prep to be done in the kitchen. The singular commitment of a scratch kitchen demands complete immersion. Frank had not cooked professionally in years. Cousin Leonard swiped some kitchen aprons, towels, and a Chef's coat—sized forty-four long—for Frank to try on from the linen storage bin.

It fit.

Cousin Leonard also set a pot of coffee on and turned the kitchen radio to the same FM station he had listened to for the last thirty years, a dreadful rotation of classic rock. He brought Frank his coffee and set down two prep sheets—a listing of commonly prepared items that the restaurant created on an as-needed basis. These were the building blocks of the menu items and they had to be made first. Frank stared at them, rusty on the abbreviated terminology of the kitchen, and wondered what he had gotten himself into.

"You really worked for the government?" Cousin Leonard asked.

"We're working for them right now, Leonard. Take a look at your paycheck. We all work for the government."

"Not me, Frank. Babe pays me in cash on 'count of my SSI disability and on 'count of my accident."

"Any word about Bobo and Jason?"

"They went to work for Lo Piccolo. They couldn't wait for Babe to reopen."

"Is Pops still around?"

"He gets in at four. He's a closer cause he can't sleep on 'count of his cancer."

"So it's me, you, and Pops."

"That's it for now. I have the word out that we're looking for a couple of guys. Hey, can I ask you a question?"

"Sure, Leonard."

"Did you work on the Government Street?"

"The what?" Frank was not trying to be sarcastic. He did not understand Cousin Leonard's question.

"You know. When I was a kid and we went to Washington, D.C., for a school bus trip, they took us down the Government Street with all the buildings. The Capitol is at one end and the pencil-shaped monument at the other."

"The Mall. You mean the National Mall?"

"I guess that's what they call it. I wouldn't call it a mall. There wasn't no Best Buy or Target or nothing like that. They had the museum there where Archie Bunker's chair was in it."

"The Smithsonian."

"I thought it was the coolest place on earth. The Government Street."

"So this prep list," Frank said, "how do you want to divvy it up?"

"Joe used to start with the stocks, if needed, then the soup and sauces. I worked downstairs on pasta and bread. After that, if Joe was running anything special for the evening he would work on that while I concentrated on the line. I'd start with the *garde manger* station, just getting it prepped up. You wouldn't believe how much salad mix we blow through and we cut and wash our own. It's an iceberg mix and it has to be held real cold to give it that pop. And then vegetables. We have a full antipasti station—six cooked, marinated, six crudo style—every night and there's a lot of work to getting that set up."

"That's a start."

"Yeah, then I'd work my way over to the hot line and get that set up, too. Joe didn't want that done until after lunch. He didn't like holding things warm for too long. He'd say that all the guys would have to do is reheat properly at night what we had cooked during the day. Joe's system was simple. Cook it the day before, let it develop in the cooler, then re-heat at night."

"What do you think happened to Joe?" Frank shot Cousin Leonard a hard glance. "What am I missing?"

"I have no idea Frank. I'm almost scared to be here without him."

"So it's me, you, and Pops tonight."

"Right."

"No specials. We'll just run with the base menu until we get our sea legs."

"I'm heading down to do bread. I'm also going to make butter, mozzarella, and ricotta," Cousin Leonard said, and then disappeared into the basement prep kitchen.

Frank stared at the prep sheets. He hung the two pages up on the dupe rack for reference. In setting up his chicken stock, he sliced an index finger at the fleshy tip while splitting some celery. The blood oozed out onto the plastic cutting board surface, the bright red ink of our human genome containing every secret and nuance of our mysterious origins.

He knew then he was all in.

He also knew how unfit and unprepared he was to be standing on his feet and preparing food. This was a young man's profession, one of outrageously long hours and relatively little pay, a path that made no sense whatsoever to those who lived outside of it, but to those on the inside there was no other way.

It was not unlike what he had just left at the CIA, except that the blood spilled here, in the kitchen, was all very local and real.

By noon Cousin Leonard reappeared from the basement kitchen. He had produced a prodigious amount of prep—easily triple the output of Frank—and he sought permission to sneak out back for a smoke.

"You don't have to ask, Leonard," Frank said. "See you out there in a second. I have to strain the stocks."

They stood out back in the parking lot, next to the Dumpster, wearing winter coats with their kitchen aprons hanging out from the bottom. Frank didn't smoke, but the cold, clean air was a welcome relief from the claustrophobic, stale air of the kitchen.

"How far did you get?" Cousin Leonard asked.

"'Bout half-way down the list."

"Not bad. You'll get the hang of it."

"We still have to make beans for the pasta fagioli."

"I'll handle that. Nobody knows the recipe, except Joe and me."

"That's what I wanted to ask you. Did Joe ever write any of his recipes down?"

"Nope. He was super-paranoid about that."

"What's the deal with Lo Piccolo? Why did those two knock heads so much?"

"Could be a lot of things."

"Well, take a guess, Leonard."

"Lo Piccolo thinks of himself as something other than a restaurant owner."

"Is he?"

"I don't think so. But he does present himself in a way that's what Joe would say was different."

"How so?"

"He's got all types of food allergies. Whenever he came in here for dinner, we had to cook plain, plain, plain for him. The fucker is allergic to tomatoes. Can you believe that? So, it's like whenever he showed up here with his entourage, we kinda had to stop everything and cook for him specially. That's how the pastina in brodo got on the menu. When Joe put it out for Lo Piccolo, he used to order it all the time. It's what his mother fed him when he was a baby—pastina in brodo—a little butter at the end and parmiggiano. And lots of ground black pepper. The king of sloppy pasta can't even eat his own sugary sauce. I heard he blew up like a balloon once when somebody put some tomato sauce inside his braciole in his own restaurant just to fuck him over."

"No shit. I wouldn't have seen that coming."

"It could have been the time Lo Piccolo came in here years back with his wife and kids. This was before Joe was famous and Lo Piccolo was sniffing around, seeing if we were doing any business. Well, Joe comes out of the kitchen and starts working the dining room. He goes to all the tables: "Good evening, how is everything tonight?" Joe used to do this song and dance in the early days. He gets to Lo Piccolo's table, looks right at Trixie Lo Piccolo and says: "Well, it nice to see you here for a change, meaning, of course, Lo Piccolo wasn't with one of his coozes."

"Nice," Frank laughed, vaguely recalling the incident.

"Yeah, that probably started it. Trixie jumped over the table and grabbed Joe. Babe jumped on top of Trixie. Lo Piccolo didn't want to soil his suit so he just sat there while his driver, Bobby Ornstein—The Hook-nosed Jew—jumped in too."

"It sounds like a game of Twister."

"Well after that incident, Lo Piccolo planted some coke on Joe down in the basement of the restaurant. It was one of our dishwashers that did it. Lo Piccolo dropped the dime to the cops, who were in on it anyways and getting paid off by Lo Piccolo to find the bag with a letter on it that said: *'Give this to Joe.'* The restaurant got some bad publicity out of it but the charges went away."

"What about this money he owed Lo Piccolo?"

"Yeah, that too. He didn't actually owe Lo Piccolo the money. He owed Lo Piccolo's card game the money."

"How much?"

"Fifty thousand, minimum. Joe was a bad card player. Lo Piccolo knew it."

"Did Babe know this?"

"Babe knows everything. That's why Joe was never allowed to handle the money. We'd have been out of business a long time ago if Joe handled the restaurant take. Whatever he made on TV and appearances he got to keep and gamble or spend away. But he could never touch the restaurant's money."

"I didn't realize he had a gambling problem."

"What do you mean, gambling problem? Joe had a card problem. He was a lousy card player. That's all. Lo Piccolo organizes a high stakes game every Monday night with a bunch of Indian doctors—the dot heads. They love to gamble. So Joe shows up one night, probably loaded, and proceeds to lose a lot of money at the table and doesn't pay up. He's good for it, though;

'cause he's Chef Joe Bass from the TV The dot heads are big fans of his. Joe keeps showing up to the game like nothing ever happened. He's riding Lo Piccolo, you see. Then Joe loses his gig on TV and his endorsements dry up, and suddenly Joe's hurting for cash. Lo Piccolo loses face 'cause he's working these Indian doctors to invest in the hotel he wants to build. He thinks there's gonna be more gambling downtown in ten years—without the Senecas, 'cause the Senecas keep telling New York State F-You—and Lo Piccolo thinks he's De Niro in Casino."

"Was Lo Piccolo capable of killing Joe?" Frank looked at Cousin Leonard, who was looking away.

"I'm not to say. Nobody should have to die the way Joe did."

"What do you mean, Leonard?"

"He was knifed, Frank. It was just such an awful mess."

Leonard smoked another cigarette while Frank looked out over the neighborhood that once bustled with activity but now remained a burnt-out shell of its former self. He had seen worse, in Beirut, in Naples, in Bosnia, and all over Russia, but this was still bad. When Leonard stamped out his second cigarette that was the signal that they were to get back to work and get ready for dinner. They had another four hours of prep before service and they were still behind.

"Joe was just yanking Lo Piccolo's chain," Leonard said when he looked at the prep list again. "He was going to pay up."

"Did you tell the police all this?

"The police," Cousin Leonard now stared at Frank. "I never told the police nothing."

"Yes, but I thought Babe..."

"Babe talked to the police. I can't talk to the police. Nobody knows I work here, except Joe, Babe, and Pops, on 'count of my accident."

"Leonard, you may have told me this before but I have forgotten. What was this accident?"

"When I was a baby they dropped me on my head."

Midway through the ragù coniglio (a rabbit sauce braised with tomato and faint scent of fennel) Frank finally found a rhythm in the kitchen for the first time and started to feel better about himself. Cousin Leonard continued to work circles around him, bouncing from one station to the next, tasting, testing and refining the *mise en place*. He moved like a giant cat or, at the very least, a veteran cook on a Great Lakes ship, toggling back and forth between stations around the galley, always slicing and dicing with blinding speed. Cousin Leonard may have been a borderline imbecile but he was no less than an idiot savant when getting the kitchen ready for service.

He blew through cases of button mushrooms, cauliflower, red and golden beets, baby artichokes, asparagus, bell peppers, roman beans, green and yellow wax beans, and carrots in record time for the antipasti table.

He peeled eggplant with a giant French knife, rotating the meaty vegetable as if it were on a swivel in the manner of Japanese chef, and perfectly sliced off discs to be grilled and marinated. He whipped up the batter for the panelle, the chickpea flour pancakes that were served with slathered on house made ricotta and olive oil.

Oh, and the potatoes. He knocked off a forty-pound box of Idahos in eight minutes flat. Half were used for buttermilk mashed, which factually contained no buttermilk at all. The secret to them was the addition of Galbani mascarpone whipped in with lots of butter, salt, and pepper—*semplice.* Chef had thought buttermilk sounded more American since it resided on that side of the menu and that's why he chose to describe them in this manner. The other half of the potatoes went to patate rosmarino and gnocchi di patate, the dish that no matter how much Cousin Leonard prepped, could not be kept in stock, they were that light and feathery on the tongue.

In fact, the menu carried few descriptions of the ingredients of the dishes at Restaurant Giueseppe Basi and that was by design. Chef was not about to share his methods with the ignorant. Taste alone would carry his cuisine; not vertical presentation, not wordy prose, not even accurate prose, were to be substituted for the one result Chef Joe Bass sought from all of his cooking—real transparency—the kind that came not from the rational part of the brain but the emotional core.

The clock crept closer to four o'clock and Frank started to panic that they would not be ready for dinner service. He expected to see Babe stroll into the kitchen at any moment in full black costume, her makeup and jewelry set perfectly, and when she did appear, more stunning than he'd anticipated, he was shocked by his adolescent desire to please her.

Then in a flourish, he watched the true roundsman talents of Cousin Leonard unleashed. It started with the short ribs—the rosticciana—then the meat loaf, the strip steaks cut and portioned, the calamari cut for frying and grilling, the clams and mussels scrubbed and put on an ice bath, meatballs, braciole and finally the lasagnette al San Giuseppe—the house specialty—came out of the oven—all in the span of twenty minutes.

"Leonard, with the exception of the prosciutto di San Danielle, I don't see any pork on this menu whatsoever," Frank noted

"Man, how long have you been gone? You know Chef never ate pork."

"I didn't know that."

"He considered it vile. Didn't your grandmother teach him that or something ? At least that's what he said."

Frank searched his memory banks for a reference. It was true that Joe Bass was privy to many more intimate discussions of food with his grandmother than he was. They spent so much time together at the stove or downstairs in the second kitchen where tomatoes were canned and baking was done, so it was entirely conceivable that pork was forbidden in the kitchen of Maria Grazia. But Frank did remember distinctly that pork found its way into their family dinner on occasion. This was, indisputably, in the manner in which Maria Grazia cooked peas. The simple frozen peas found at the grocery store were transformed by the addition of diced pork and paprika. Come to think of it, Frank thought, peas were the only dish that called for onion, too.

There was a loud report at the kitchen door. Cousin Leonard and Frank looked up in startled unison.

"Open up," Babe screamed from the outside. "Open this door right now!"

Cousin Leonard sprang over a stack of empty cardboard cases to open the kitchen door.

"It's Pops," Babe said, panting from the cold air. "I found him in a snow bank. It looks like he's been beaten."

Frank rushed out the back door and ran to the edge of the parking lot. The splayed body of Julio "Pops" DeSimone was resting on the top of a mass of snow four feet high. A stream of blood from the left side of his face had made its way onto the white snow.

"Pops, can you hear me?" Frank asked. He checked for a pulse, found it, then checked Pops's eyes.

They were dazed.

He didn't want to move him and started to take his cell phone out of his pocket when Cousin Leonard reached over and lifted Pops up and slung him over his back.

"I'm getting him out of the snow. He's got no immune system."

Pops remained prone on the carpet of the restaurant when he regained consciousness. The bleeding had resulted from an offense to the left temporal lobe of his skull, opening a two centimeter gash. It was arrested by application of styptic from the restaurant's first aid kit. Chef had been a stickler for keeping that first aid kit full and replenished. He had even designated its maintenance as an official prep item to do. He never wanted someone bleeding in his restaurant without a means to stop it, and a small container of cayenne pepper was placed in the kit, at Chef's insistence, in case the styptic ran out.

"I'm late," Pops said, shaking his head. "Where are we at, Leonard?"

"It's OK, Pops," Cousin Leonard said. "What happened?"

"I got popped."

"Pops, you got popped."

They all laughed nervously as Pops DeSimone regained lucidity.

"Do you know by who?" Babe leaned over with a warm towel that she applied to his face.

"The Hook-nosed Jew—Bobby Ornstein. He got me good."

"Mother..." Babe murmured.

"Yeah, I cabbed it down here and stopped at the store for some smokes. When I came out, I noticed this car pulling along side of me. Hook-nose gets out and starts walking in front of me. He's a gangly fuck, ain't he? Tells me not to even bother going to work. That this restaurant wasn't going to be around much longer. I wasn't bothered. There's nothing a Hook-nosed Jew can say to a man with stage two pancreatic cancer that's gonna bother him."

"I'm calling the police," Frank said. "We need to get Pops looked at and get charges against this guy."

They all looked at Frank strangely.

"Frank, what the fuck?" Pops said. "I got popped. I didn't say I got fucked in the ass. There's no need for a rape kit. Leonard, please gimme an apron and a cup of coffee. I'm going to sit upright for ten minutes and then I'll be back there to put it out. We are opening tonight? That is the plan?"

"Yes, Pops," Babe said, kissing his forehead and then his cheeks. "That is the plan."

EIGHT

Like a tsunami, there is no reliable warning system to detect the tidal wave of humanity that can hit a restaurant at an uncertain hour such as the first hour of the re-opening of Restaurant Giuseppe Basi. What was supposed to be a soft opening for friends and family turned into a full-fledged assault on the restaurant's square footage, as table after table filled up and turned with no apparent end in sight.

This was the community's outpouring of support for Babe La Bruna. They had been denied access to Chef Joe Bass's funeral but when word spread that this was *the* night, they came out in droves—in four tops, eight tops, six tops, twelve tops—and Babe ushered them all in with hugs, tears, and laughter.

The waiting list stretched two hours long. The restaurant was slammed. They came to see and be seen. A legend had passed all too early and this was their communal expression of grief. They stood three-deep at the bar. And still they kept coming in without complaint. They needed confirmation that the restaurant was intact. That their favorite server—the brunette with the tight ass, the red head with the big jugs, the busboy with the salami stuffed in his pants—were all still there. That Billy Cruickshank was behind the bar, pouring side cars, martinis, and bellinis, and telling Billy Cruickshank -type jokes—*Hey, so there's a mick, dago and a Jew stranded on a desert island.*

Babe took it all in from her perch at the hostess station. The crowd had confirmed her deeply held belief that she was selling sex more than food, and the front of the house looked very sexy at this moment. You don't sell sex in a restaurant by taking reservations. That was prostitution. Restaurant Giuseppe Basi did not take reservations. The controlled chaos that enveloped the restaurant now had rendered a debaucherous result. But still, there were other questions to be answered.

Would the pasta fagioli taste the same?

That answer came early and often.

"It's great, Babe. Perfect. It's just the same—well nothing is the same without Joe—but it was superb."

Babe came into the kitchen to check on Frank after the first rush. After a rocky start on his second ticket of the evening (a deceptively simple yet difficult-to-execute six top that required six different appetizers, six different entrees and then a chef's sampling of the entire menu on small plates), Bruno found a sense of calm and resolve that he could handle the sauté station.

In such a lean kitchen, the sauté station was the equivalent of the captain's chair or, to borrow a sporting analogy, the quarterback position. Frank oversaw the orders as they came in real time, hand-written on dupes by the servers. Restaurant Giuseppe Basi was not an automated operation with a point of sale computer system like the majority of restaurants.

This, too, was by design.

Once the order was placed on the rack, Frank picked it up and called it out to Cousin Leonard, working the grill and fryer, and Pops, working the *garde manger* (the cold station). He racked the dupe in right-to-left fashion, meaning the newest order was placed on the right while older orders stretched to the left, so he could scan the breadth of what was due, and read in the Semitic tradition of Hebrew and Arabic.

"Working two San Giuseppes, one potato gnocchi, two ricotta gnocchi, for table six. Table seventeen has two meatloaf dinners, one steak, a pappardelle with rabbit, and Pops, I need salads for that table now, please."

The success of the kitchen depended on the sauté station's ability to traffic, coordinate, forecast, and narrate the flow of orders. Frank was part cheerleader, part bad-cop (Leonard—a shade longer on the calamari. It's too light.), and full-time expediter. He was also responsible for cooking everything that came over the eight burners of the restaurant's one Vulcan stove and this was a heavy burden of pasta, pasta, and more pasta.

"Don't over-sauce the fusilli," Cousin Leonard said, watching Frank plate his first Fusilli Calabrese. "Cardinal rule of this restaurant—don't over-sauce. They want more sauce, we serve it to them on the side."

"Acknowledged," Frank shouted, as his first jolt of kitchen adrenaline kicked in, "but please, Cousin Leonard, no more references to cardinals. They're all crooks."

The only sauté dish that continued to confound Frank for the entire evening was the egg foo yung. Its presence on the menu was an anomaly to anyone unfamiliar with the practicum of Chef Joe Bass.

Convinced that it was the curative for a hangover, Joe Bass would cross the border to Niagara Falls, Ontario, after a night out of drinking and eat this dish at his favorite little Chinese hole-in-the-wall restaurant operated by immigrants from Zhejiang Province. When he finally established enough of a rapport and credibility with the owners, Chef asked to see how the egg foo yung was made and he was immediately escorted into the kitchen for a tutorial.

Chef ignored all pleas from Babe and the staff to the contrary and put egg foo yung on his menu. He adapted the version taught to him across the border and eliminated the pork component. Instead, he substituted diced chuck, resisted the temptation to add green onions, and went with bean sprouts, water chestnuts, and celery as the *sofrito* of the dish before he added an *à la minute* dice of vegetable scraps from the antipasti prep to put his version of egg foo yung over the top.

He doctored his salsa bruna (brown sauce)—adding a zing of colatura di alici to it—and served the final plated dish straight up as an omelet, or St. Louis-style, between two slices of crustless white bread, with mayo, lettuce and a pickle.

And therein lay the problem to Frank's understanding of how to execute it. This was an egg dish, cracked to order, and as any experienced line cook will tell you, it is easy thing to screw up eggs over an open flame, especially when you are slammed with forty other tickets demanding your attention.

"Your sauté pan is too hot," Cousin Leonard said when Frank shouted his exasperation over the first order of egg foo yung that came back from the dining room.

"Is this dish really necessary? We are buried here and I'm supposed to crack eggs and make an omelet?"

"Chef put it on for exactly this reason," Cousin Leonard smiled. "You can't make egg foo yung on a busy night, you can't work at this restaurant. Chef did it. Taught me. I taught Bobo. He taught Jason. I'll teach you. Lower the heat to your pan and start over."

Finally, the kitchen surrendered after three complete turns of the dining room because they had simply run out of food to serve. Normally, this would have been considered a most heinous kitchen offense, but since this was their first night back, the mood amongst the staff was one of jubilation. Even Pops, with a bandage over his forehead, stage two cancer in his pancreas and spreading, moved fluently about the kitchen.

Frank looked up at the clock. It was his fifteenth hour on his feet and he had another solid two more to go of cleaning and getting ready for the next day. So this is what real work feels like, he thought, and began assembling his produce list to be called into the vendor that night for delivery the next day.

Two police detectives walked through the kitchen door, one of which Frank recognized immediately.

"Did you text me?" Detective Nathan Sensabaugh asked Frank.

"Hello Detective. Glad you could make it, " Frank said. "Please give us a moment to get finished up here and I'll be right with you."

They met in the cubbyhole in the kitchen; a closet-sized office for receiving orders and processing vendor payments, after Frank removed his apron and chef's coat.

"Gentlemen, one of our employees was attacked here tonight, outside on his way into work. He was lumped up pretty good and we know who did it."

"This is becoming quite a violent place, Mr. Bruno," Detective Sensabaugh said.

"I don't know the guy but he goes by the name of Hooknose."

"Bobby Ornstein."

"You know him?"

"Mr. Bruno, what's not to know? The only Jew in

this town who's over six-five. He's the cantor over at Temple Beth El and supposedly has a decent voice. I wouldn't know; I'm not Jewish."

"I'd have never guessed. You can call me Frank. You had mentioned a print you were able to photograph outside the kitchen door the day my cousin was murdered."

"OK."

"I'm thinking there might be a print like that out in the snow bank where our employee was dumped."

"Frank Bruno, right? I looked you up. Very impressive. I do background checks for FBI clearances part-time. It's good money," Detective Sensabaugh said. "You have the highest security clearance I've ever come across in twenty years of doing these checks, but this, sir, this is Niagara Falls. This is not CSI. You want us to interview Bobby Ornstein, just say so. We'll bring him in."

"I want you to do something. It's been six weeks."

"Sir, let's examine the facts. Your cousin, the famous Chef Joe Bass, suffered a catastrophic stab wound to his coronary artery. It was estimated that he lived less than ten minutes after he was stabbed, and that was pretty much him flailing away trying to get to his cell phone right here in this office. Murder weapon? Take a look around. This place is full of cutlery that fits the bill except that when we examined the kitchen we found the entire set of kitchen knives to be in the dishwasher—washed, rinsed, and sanitized."

"You check the dishwasher levers for prints?"

"We are not incompetent, Mr. Bruno. Hard to believe this is so, but yes we checked. We checked the entire kitchen for prints. We extracted fifteen sets of unique prints, twelve of them belonging to employees of this restaurant, three unknown. Now let's move on to motive. Any idea who might want to kill your cousin?"

"No idea."

"Well let's start with all the people he either owed money to or he had pissed off."

"The list is long?"

"Very long. We know—or should say we heard—that he was banned from the casino. He had lost a lot of cash at the tables and had a hard time paying up. We think he owed Bebe Lo Piccolo money but Lo Piccolo is more or less a hobbyist."

"Meaning?"

"He's just not what he portrays himself as."

"Yes, but what about Ornstein? I heard Ornstein works for Lo Piccolo and I saw what he did to one of our guys. That was very real."

"Ornstein is a Jewjene."

"A Jewjene?"

"It's a Jew who thinks he's Italian. More specifically, Italian-American."

"Are you going to interview him? I want him charged."

"We'll interview him, sir, but your employee has to come forward and press charges or at least show up and identify him in a lineup."

"I'll have him there."

"I'm guessing not. Not from this crew."

"What about the door being opened? You said the kitchen door was open the morning Joe was killed."

"That could mean several things. We know Joe opened the door to vent the restaurant from the gas smell. We have established that."

"And this is a lousy neighborhood."

"It's seen better days. That we will grant. But there was no evidence of a robbery. Mrs. La Bruna did not report anything missing. Your cousin had a wad of bills on him that were removed by the coroner. Did he have a drug problem?"

"Not that I know of."

"Neither do we. He seems clean in that regard or at least we will allow a variance for recreational use as is par with this industry. So the chances of someone coming in from that back door and killing him appear remote, in our opinion. I should say stab your cousin because whoever did it was allowed to get very close to him. Wouldn't you say?"

"Someone from the restaurant?"

"Perhaps. We did verify that Mrs. La Bruna was at the bank that morning. She was positively identified by the teller and bank manager and we have the video to confirm it. Anyone else, Mr. Bruno, that you could think of that might be in this restaurant that morning?"

Frank had always been in the position of asking question and not answering them during an interrogation. He thought he knew where this was going but he was going to let Detective Sensabaugh get there on his own time. It didn't make sense.

"Not that I can think of," Frank said, committing his first act of civilian perjury, for whatever reason was not clear to him.

"That Babe La Bruna is a pretty cold fish wouldn't you say, Mr. Bruno? I mean here she is prancing around six weeks after her husband's murder, open for business as usual."

"I wouldn't say business as usual, Detective."

"Oh, really. How would they write it up at Langley?"

"Detective, you are violating your protocol with regard to your part-time security clearance screening gig. What does that net you, 10 K a year? You've already got your twenty in on the force. The state pension on top of the fed pension when you hang it up. You're bullet proof. You ready to Ted Kazinkski-it-up at your hunting cabin and wait for 2012?"

"Very funny, Mr. Bruno. No, I think I'll stick around and get some of Chef Joe Bass's famous broccoli parm."

"Sorry kitchen's closed."

"What's up, Pops?" Detective Sensabaugh ignored Frank for the moment. "Hook-nose slapped you around; you call him a kike or something?"

"Yeah, I told him he sings like Lady GaGa," Pops DeSimone grinned.

"I'll bring in the Jewjene," Detective Sensabaugh addressed Frank again. "But you tell Babe La Bruna we are going to have to sit down and have an adult conversation. Sooner, rather than later."

NINE

Shortly after their initial meeting in D.C., Hayden Buckingham began sexting Frank Bruno.

It was not sexting in the usual salacious call-and-response mode, but more of a cornucopia of images of Buckingham next to ingredients found at New York's Greenmarket, or dinner at a famous four-star restaurant, or coffee and note-taking with a celebrity chef. The images progressively became more erotic in the depiction, not just of food, but of Hayden fondling, frisking, and eventually inserting food into non-traditional food consuming orifices.

Frank was not certain why he was the recipient of these sexts, but nevertheless found himself fascinated with the trappings of a high priestess of the Food Universe.

There was the Buckingham Conference on sustainable heirloom vegetables that she chaired at Cornell

University's School of Agriculture, receiving top billing as a returning distinguished alum, albeit from the lowly School of Communications.

She blurbed Barbara Kingsolver's follow up to *Animal, Vegetable, Miracle* with a first-position quotation on the back cover; her printed quote reading quite different from the original one she had submitted to Kingsolver's publisher: *Squat, Pee, Wipe.*

"Kingsolver's follow-up is the most important read of the new year. It will literally make you rethink your relationship with food. Make time for this book and for food."

There was her appearance on *Iron Chef* where she judged Battle Turnip between Masahiro Morimoto and some molecular gastronomy geek from Chicago whose entire crew wore red bandannas in the manner of a street gang and sported an excessive amount of tattoos and body piercings. Hayden Buckingham had cleared her now well-reported line with the segment producer of *Iron Chef* before she actually delivered it at the Kitchen Stadium judging table—*Morimoto you dress and cook like a Yakuza pimp and we are all your bitches.*

A standing ovation in Kitchen Stadium went not to the victor Morimoto in Battle Turnip, but to Hayden Buckingham, when she admonished the molecular gangstas from Chicago to stop wearing those silly bandanas, take a collective shower, and learn how to cook without their little science kits because their bodies stank, their food stank, and she was not going to put up with this bullshit anymore.

But no matter where she went, or what she said, or what she wrote about, the one question that dogged Hayden was that of the fate of Chef Joe Bass.

At first, she did not have much to say in this regard and it had started to bother her. Having created the character of Chef Joe Bass in her writing, she was bound and determined to write the final chapter. That was also when the sext messages to Frank became more graphic.

There were only so many ways you could go when writing about food, Hayden surmised. The conventional route of that of a restaurant critic or a food writer/blogger and historian required one to become an endless consumer. This was not appealing to her since she believed it led to a path of mental disturbance from the consumption of too many calories, too many meals, and too much idle time seeking ways in which to describe things as precious that are not precious at all, such as the commercial preparation of food.

The other path was to begin a series of written pieces and television appearances about food in the first person. Anthony Bourdain had figured this out with his first book years ago, after he had also figured out that he was less of a chef and more of a reformed druggie with a particular sense of humor that appealed to other reformed druggies, many of whom happened to be chefs.

More power to you, Anthony Bourdain.

Hayden Buckingham was reaching for some twist of

career fate similar to Bourdain's and that of her two most cherished American writers of the second half of the twentieth century—Norman Mailer and Truman Capote—when she pitched her concept to executives from the Discovery Channel of the video version of *The Buck Stopped Here;* a first-person, no-holds-barred look behind the curtains of American restaurants.

Boned: The Life and Death of Chef Giuseppe Basi was to be the test vehicle.

Her timing was perfect.

The Discovery Channel was suffering from crab fisherman fatigue when their white trash cast of the *Deadliest Catch* stopped production over a pay dispute. Captain Numbnuts and his crew of crabbers were locked out of the studio while Hayden was given the green light to shoot a pilot.

Pitching was the easy part. Now she had to deliver the goods.

Frank did not delude himself into thinking that the pornographic images in the message box of his cell phone were anything other than Hayden's cultivation of his confidence. He was not on the operations side of things at the CIA except in rare instances. He was an analyst. But he did understand the basic routine of asset acquisition. Buckingham's sexting was an intuitive Tour de Force use of just such a methodology.

Still, it was one thing to recognize what was going on and still yet another to become immutable to it. Frank was brought nearly to climax by one particular image—Hayden Buckingham forcibly choked from behind by another woman whose strap-on appeared targeted in the right direction; her one leg suspended on a prep table and her platform heels—a clear violation of sanitary kitchen practices—spiking through a fresh slice of brioche. The woman with the strap-on seemed familiar to him, as did the kitchen setting. She wore a black leather singlet, cheekies, elbow-length leather gloves, and her jet-black hair provided the most compelling pixilation of the entire digitized image.

Clearly, Frank had been mistaken.

From the looks of things, Babe La Bruna was in charge of everything—front of the house and back of the house—that went on in Restaurant Giuseppe Basi.

"This was just sent to me," Frank said, holding his iPhone up to Babe, who was in her office counting the proceeds from the past evening and readying the deposit.

"Yeah, that was a couple of years ago," Babe barely looked up from her counting. "We used to have a lot of fun."

"Did Joe know about this?"

"Who do you think was taking the pictures? Heavens, as soon as that Flip camera came out, I thought Joe had lost his mind and wanted to become a porn director or something."

"Babe, I'm not feeling real comfortable with the way things are going here. I mean it's been great being back home and all. It was the mental vacation I needed, but something just doesn't feel right."

"Frank, you were always a bit of a nerd when it came to sex. Does this," she said, holding up his iPhone with the image of her and Hayden, "scare you?"

"I check for blood every time I have my morning constitutional. That's what scares me."

"You and your family's obsession with elimination. Joe was the exact same way."

"Well, it's all part of the same cycle of the food business."

"Buckingham wants to come to the restaurant and film us for some TV show she's producing," Babe said, putting the cash deposit into a cloth bag. "She wants you to fall in love with her. It's the way she works. That way she thinks you'll do anything for her to get the shots she wants. I saw it happened with Joe. He was like a puppy in her presence—Sit up, Chef... Down, Chef... Bring me food, Chef...Chef, lick my asshole."

"When is this happening?"

"Next week. It could be good for us, Frank. We shoot it now, it makes it onto the air in a couple months, and it starts getting played heavily right about the time the tourist season starts to gear up. We'll be through the winter and the slow months."

"Aren't you just the nifty media strategist?"

"What's that supposed to mean?"

"Joe's been dead for a few months and you seem to have fully recovered."

Babe stared quizzically at Frank.

"And your point being?"

"Babe, it's not what I would have expected from you."

"Now what would that be?"

"That you killed Joe. I just didn't think you had that type of thing in you."

"The only reason I would have killed Joe would be to have a weeknight off. Believe me, I thought about it. But do you think I could trust this place to run with anyone else, especially my recalcitrant husband, the great Chef Joe Bass?"

"It doesn't seem like you needed him anymore, anyway."

"So what would be the point in killing him?"

"I don't know. You said you were at the bank when Cousin Leonard called."

"Why don't you just waterboard me?" Babe stared at Frank. "Or hook me up to one of the those machines. You must have a few friends in the business. I'll take a test. Set it up. I'll take a test."

"And what happened when Leonard called you?"

"Why don't you ask Leonard; and after that you can get the fuck out of this restaurant."

"Let's not get so riled up, Babe. Just sit back and tell me what happened again. I need to understand things."

"I'll tell you anything you want to know. I went out to make the deposit that morning. Leonard called me while I was standing in line at the commercial window of the bank. He said Joe was hurt again and I needed to come back to the restaurant. He didn't say that he had been stabbed. He didn't say he was bleeding. He just said to come back. Then, when I got there, I saw Joe and the blood and I called the police immediately."

"Was Leonard there?"

"Of course he was there. He was shaking and mumbling. I was screaming at him and asking him what happened."

"When the police arrived, was Leonard there?"

"I don't remember. I was pressing down on Joe's chest with a kitchen towel. He was barely responsive."

"What was Leonard doing?"

"I honestly don't remember. I rode with Joe in the ambulance. They worked on him for almost two hours but they told me Joe had actually died before he even arrived at the hospital."

"We need to talk to Leonard again."

"Leonard didn't kill Joe, Frank. Leonard idolized him. The police have interviewed him two times already."

"That's not what Leonard said. Did they ask what he was doing at the restaurant?"

"I told them he was our porter and a relative. That he came in the morning, did the cleaning, and we paid him off the books."

"Has Leonard ever been in trouble?"

"Not to my knowledge. Frank, he goes to church with his mother. He's forty years old and sleeps in the same bed that he grew up in. He drinks now and then but I've never seen him raise a hand in anger at anyone."

"Neither have I. So why didn't you tell the police that he works here?"

"I did tell them he works here. I just didn't get into the part about him cooking here. You know his situation. Ever since he was sixteen, he's been collecting SSI disability. He started right before Reagan changed the rules. I'd estimate that between that and the money he makes in cash he has a couple hundred K hidden somewhere."

"Then if it wasn't Leonard, it was someone who came through that back door and nothing about that makes sense."

"Suppose someone came here to rob the place and Joe surprised them. That's what I think."

"The police say Joe had a wad of cash on him at the time and that it wasn't touched."

"I said came here to rob the place, not rob Joe. Joe was almost never here anymore. Anyone who had studied this restaurant knew that he almost never was here. Come here, I want to show you something," Babe stood up from her desk and walked out of the basement office.

She walked over to the room that at one time had been the embalming room of the Magaddino funeral parlor but had now been converted into a fully-equipped second kitchen, complete with a full suite of equipment, including a dough mixer, pasta machine, tilt kettle, convection oven, work tables, and combo walk-in cooler/freezer.

She opened the door to the walk-in cooler and Frank followed behind her. She walked to the back of the cooler and opened another door that led to an attached freezer. The sub-zero air hit Frank like a sledgehammer. Babe moved a few rolling racks with cases of frozen lamb shanks and cases of boxed frozen meat bones around until the bare aluminum wall of the freezer was exposed. She then put her hands on the metal lined interior of the freezer wall and another door—this one without a handle or markings—opened to yet another passageway.

She turned on the light to a concrete-walled room measuring less than one hundred square feet total. There was a single air duct bringing in fresh oxygen from the outside. The room was lined with metro shelving, the ubiquitous adjustable metal shelving used in restaurants and foodservice operations for storage. On the shelves sat bundles of shrink-wrapped Canadian currency and black metal boxes similar to those used as safety deposit boxes.

"Isn't this amazing?" Babe La Bruna asked. "Old Man Magaddino used to count his money right here. When the feds arrested him in the early seventies they found over 400 K in his back yard. They say there was triple that amount right here in this room."

"What's with the Canadian money?"

"Sixty percent of our business is Canadian. Now, I'm not talking about during the tourism season, I'm talking year-round. When we first opened the restaurant the Canadian dollar was worth about half of what the U.S. dollar was worth. But this town is so dead that Joe didn't want to turn anybody away so he started accepting Canadian money at par. Think of that? If you came in here back in those days, you were getting a near 50% discount on your meal. But then, the Canadians were the only customers that were coming in here."

"What's in the metal boxes?"

"Gold."

"Gold?"

"Yes I started buying gold five years ago with some of the Canadian cash up in Toronto and bringing it over in the car. I first started reading about currencies when Joe finally sprung for the Internet connection in our office. He would have never done it if it weren't so convenient to batch out the credit cards. Then he wanted to check on the horse races and I wanted to keep track of our accounts online. Do you realize how much the Canadian dollar has appreciated in the last five years?"

Frank stared around at the shelving. He was dumbfounded. He tried to do the math in his head but Babe interrupted him.

"It's a million five and change, if you're trying to figure it out," she said.

"What's with the cases of dry Good Seasons Italian mix on the top shelf?"

"Ah, now you know all of our secrets at Restaurant Giuseppe Basi. That's the secret ingredient to the pasta fagioli."

"You're kidding me."

"I am not. I think that if it came down to what was in this room in a fire, Joe would have grabbed the Good Seasons first. He came upon it by accident when he was fooling around one day. Chefs have a weird perversion with mass-produced, processed food items. They're like crack to most chefs. It fascinates them in a different way. Joe used to like the weirdest products, take them into the kitchen, and try and go completely "off-label" with them as he said."

"That's brilliant."

"That was Joe. He would not allow garlic or onions into anything he cooked. Sometimes, he'd make something and we'd beg him to add a little garlic, just a touch. We'd tell him to heat it in the pan then discard it the way it's done in Italy for a lot of recipes, but he wouldn't listen."

Frank had traveled the world over as a bit actor on life's grand stage, and in that time it occurred to him that Babe and Joe were busy toiling away in relative obscurity and anonymity, building a nest egg of more cash than he would ever see in a lifetime. They were devoid of political opinions, disengaged from the supposed 'real world,' unconcerned about the great sweep of human history.

"I think whomever killed Joe knew about this room," she said. "They may not have known what exactly was in here but they knew that it was here. Lo Piccolo knew it was here. Others did, too."

"Good Seasons dry mix Italian dressing. That is twisted," Frank said, laughing.

"Do you have any perversions, Frank? Anything you'd care to share with an old friend?" Babe laughed, too.

Frank felt Babe's breath upon him. It was the same throaty voice that had first wound up his adolescent coil. The room was below 50 degrees Fahrenheit but not below 45, a perfect temperature for interrogation. Babe's nipples protruded from her sweater, a genuine, honest-to-goodness, titty hard-on, the sight of which ratcheted Frank adolescent coil even tighter. He momentarily fantasized about waterboarding her but for other reasons.

"Maybe so. Maybe once."

"Tell me."

"Maybe I'd like to choke you out."

Ten

Piccolo Mondo restaurant—all 17,500 square feet of it—arose out of a corn field across the street from the Niagara Falls International Airport back in the early sixties when newly-arrived George Joseph emigrated from the Levant, married a local girl named Greta Lo Piccolo, and took her surname before opening his Italian restaurant, a factory of canned sauce and spaghetti served on ten-inch plates.

It was a dicey play for this Lebanese entrepreneur who had earned his stripes as a crafty accountant and collections agent for various members of the Buffalo mob, who, in turn, were under the direction of none other than Stefano Magaddino, the former owner of the property that now housed Restaurant Giuseppe Basi.

George Lo Piccolo wagered that the Niagara Falls Airport would become a major hub of transatlantic tourist activity.

How could it not?

It had one of the largest runways in North America capable of landing jumbo jets. The monstrous Bell Aerospace factory stood adjacent to it, as did the Air Force's 914th Air Refueling Wing. In between those two monstrosities sat a vast tract of developable land that would fit perfectly in helping to make the Niagara Falls Airport rival any airport in North America.

And of course, there are the waterfalls that, from the moment Father Louis Hennepin viewed them while exploring New France in 1680, had attracted a steady stream of European Caucasians to their banks to witness one of the world's great wonders. Trips to view the Falls of Niagara had been written about since the advent of travel literature, and the impending boom in air travel during the fifties and sixties promised to dwarf all other periods of interest in the Falls as a tourist destination combined.

George Lo Piccolo's acquisition and location of his restaurant in such close proximity to the airport seemed as close to a sure thing as possible. But even he underestimated the sheer amount of corruption and shenanigans in the City of Niagara Falls, New York, that drove any further development of the airport forty miles to an eastern suburb of Buffalo; to a landlocked municipal airport that was incapable of servicing the new brand of transcontinental aircraft that connected Europe and Asia to North America.

It was a monumental boneheaded move of political folly, stupidity, and graft.

Instead of directly connecting Niagara Falls to the major capitals of Europe and Asia, air travelers instead had to fly first to New York, then board a commuter flight to Buffalo, and then take a bus or drive the final twenty five miles west to the Falls. Those last twenty miles were more treacherous than the thousands that preceded them, since tourist traffic was deliberately re-routed through the densest and most confusing commercial boulevards of the city in an attempt to fleece every dollar away from the forlorn and frustrated travelers.

George Lo Piccolo seethed at the lost opportunity of his seemingly brilliant real estate play. But, not to be defeated, he vowed to make Piccolo Mondo a destination second only to the Falls of Niagara themselves, and committed his entire life to adding square footage onto his restaurant with the help of his only son, Bebe, who by fourteen was donning a tuxedo, a ruffled shirt and polished pair of wing tips every night while running the front of the house.

It was the advent of the packaged dinner—and the demise of the competing smorgasbord concept—that truly propelled Piccolo Mondo to profitability. George Lo Piccolo bet against the smorgasbord (too much food cost, too much waste), and instead instituted an aggressive package dinner campaign for just about every occasion that a tourist or average citizen of Niagara Falls could pull up a chair to and enjoy.

The cash register at Piccolo Mondo never stopped ringing.

If your school, church, club, workplace, fraternity, sorority, sports team, Boy Scout, or Girl Scout troop had any reason, whatsoever, to host a banquet, Piccolo Mondo had a package dinner that fit your budget. And your package dinner always concluded with orange sherbet served at no additional charge.

George Lo Piccolo considered sherbet to be one of America's greatest innovations since it transformed the unpronounceable classic sorbet into a popular dessert choice that was produced with less than 3% milk fat—a true restaurant operator's food cost wet dream. Every time George Lo Piccolo watched his service staff scoop out orange sherbet into three ounce glass vessels at the conclusion of a banquet, his blood pressure dropped nearly forty points and he knew he would live to fight another day.

It was Bebe Lo Piccolo, however, who developed the lucrative wedding business for Piccolo Mondo. Bebe parlayed Niagara Falls' status as Honeymoon Capital of America, along with the advent of wall-to-wall carpeting and the concept of the non-denominational service/reception all in one room, into a bonanza of new revenue for the restaurant.

They could not build additions to Piccolo Mondo fast enough to accommodate the increased wedding traffic. The first room—The Golfo Di Sorrento—was barely open before the next room—The Golfo Di Napoli—was under construction. George Lo Piccolo was so proud of his son's marketing instincts and savvy that he deeded him the restaurant on Bebe's thirtieth birthday.

George Lo Piccolo fantasized of an early retirement, dividing time between his grandchildren and trips back to the Levant to prune the fig trees on family land there. That fantasy came to an abrupt end when he was murdered on one such a trip to his homeland by roadside bandits that pumped an entire clip of ammunition from an Uzi into his vehicle. His wife Greta was also slain in what would have been their fortieth year of marriage. But not before George Lo Piccolo had commissioned a bronze sculptural reproduction of Charles C. Ebbets's *New York Construction Workers during the thirties over New York City* for the front entrance to Piccolo Mondo's vast four hundred-spot parking lot, serviced by a small army of valets.

If you counted closely you realized that there was a twelfth construction worker added to Ebbets's original crew of eleven, in this life-like sculptural depiction that took a local artist nearly two years to complete. That extra worker was none other than George Lo Piccolo himself, suspended on the I-beam alongside the other workers in perpetuity, at the front entrance to what was once just a cornfield. George Lo Piccolo was not eating a sandwich like the others. He was chowing down on a bowl of orange sherbet.

Outwardly, Piccolo Mondo continued to experience yearly double-digit growth (even in the financial calamity of '08–'09 when Bebe Lo Piccolo took decisive action and slashed the base price of his dinner packages by twenty percent) and the restaurant continued to grow. Volume was up, margins down, but one of the pressing problems facing Piccolo Mondo was the fact that they were running out of gulfs after which to name their new banquet rooms.

The Golfo di Salerno room was retrofitted with flatscreen monitors, wireless routers, and all the other whiz bang display technology needed to secure the pharmaceutical dinners hosted by drug reps from Big Pharma, but after that Bebe Lo Piccolo might have to scour a map of Mexico to name his next party room, whose blueprints were pinned to the walls of his office.

The other problem that confronted Lo Piccolo was the two men in his office at the present moment from the Department of Taxation and Finance of New York State. Special investigators Rodney Maltesta and Richard Vilsack had shown up to Piccolo Mondo unannounced and caught Lo Piccolo in his office before he could attempt to divert them to the Golfo di Catania room while calling his lawyer and accountant.

"How do you pronounce your last name?" Bebe Lo Piccolo asked, examining the business cards sitting on his desk.

"Vilsack."

"Ballsack?"

"Vilsack."

"Ballsack."

"Mr. Lo Piccolo, believe it or not, I've heard that one before. It was probably in the eighth grade." Special Investigator Richard Vilsack said. "We'd like to speak frankly with you and let you know that your operations are being audited by our offices."

"You pricks run up billions of dollars in deficits and you think you can balance the state budget by auditing small businesses."

"No, Mr. Lo Piccolo," Agent Rodney Maltesta said. "But we can close the revenue gap. There's a serious gap in the state between taxes owed and taxes collected."

"Maltesta, huh? Do you know what that name means in Italian? It means shithead."

"Sir. We are here simply here as a courtesy to inform you of your situation, and to offer you a deal of sorts."

"What kind of deal?"

At the sound of the word deal, Bebe Lo Piccolo was finally able to exhale.

"You can help us identify other operators from which we can close this revenue gap," Agent Vilsack said.

"You want me to sing?"

"Like a canary, Mr. Lo Piccolo," Agent Maltesta said. "I hear you have a black guy making your sauce these days."

"Chef Bobo Watson. What about him? He joined us from one the finest restaurants in the region, Restaurant Giuseppe Basi."

"A recent homicide investigation at that address yielded some information that came to our attention," Agent Vilsack said, referring to his notes. "Do you know a Barbara La Bruna?"

"We have met on social occasions."

"With your years of experience in the business, do you think you could help us identify areas of an operation—such as the one operated by Ms. La Bruna—that might be hard to decipher?"

"Decipher?"

"Yes, it appears this restaurant is a manual operation."

"I'm totally automated. I have a POS system in every room here at the restaurant. You can take a look for yourself if you don't believe me."

"We believe you, sir. We plan on looking at your system. We already subpoenaed all of your vendors for all of your invoices. Especially the ones you paid cash to. You know how many trips you took to Restaurant Depot last year. Take a guess."

"Tell me, shithead."

"Two hundred fifty-seven trips. That's a lot of cash purchases. I wonder how many of those invoices are going to show up on our audit."

"Do you know Norman Panepinto from Stormin' Norman's House of Sauce?" Agent Vilsack continued to read from his notes.

"Yes."

"Nelson Tabone of Neddy's House of Spaghetti?"

"Yes."

"Alfredo Cuneo of Da Alfredo?"

"Yes."

"Pietro Prato from A Mano?"

"Yes."

"That's the whole shooting match," Agent Maltesta turned to his colleague and winked. "I told you this was our guy."

"Mr. Lo Piccolo, in return for your cooperation and helping us to examine these operators we might be able to help you reduce the total amount of your indebtedness to the state and spare you any jail time."

"Jail time?"

"Yes, Mr. Lo Piccolo. What are your annual sales?"

"Twelve million. It says so right there on my tax returns. Look it up."

"It's been our experience with a yearly volume such as that, you're probably looking at a conservative assessment of two to three million dollars, and that's before we come in with the forensic pencil necks."

"You're like the mob!" Lo Piccolo blurted out.

"We're worse," Agent Maltesta said. "We are New York State. The Empire State."

"What do you want from me?"

"You can help us save time, Mr. Lo Piccolo," Agent Vilsak said. "Help us identify where these guys buy their products, how many people they pay off the books, where they get the liquor and beer that's not from licensed distributors. You can help us with tax-exempt certificates and other operator dirty tricks. You can tell us about their property, their spouses, their spending habits, their vacations and second homes. There are lots of ways you can cooperate and reduce that assessment."

"I'm calling my lawyer."

"Go right ahead, Mr. Lo Piccolo," Agent Maltesta said. "I just need to ask you one more thing."

"What's that?'

"How you gonna pull off having a black guy at the *Sauce Off?"*

Agent Rodney Maltesta was referring to the upcoming *Sauce Off,* the largest annual fundraiser for the American Cancer Society that pitted the area's most popular Italian-American restaurants in a 'friendly' competition to determine who had the best tomato sauce. It would also mark the first time in over a decade that Restaurant Giuseppe Basi would participate in the event. Lo Piccolo looked down at his desk, a cornered man in the four corners of his own office.

"He'll be backstage," Lo Piccolo said, referring to his African-American Executive Head Chef Harold Gildersleeve 'Bobo' Watson. "Back where nobody can see him."

The first call Lo Piccolo placed after the agents left his office was not to his attorney, Kenneth Weinstein, or his accountant, Morris Weinstein and brother of Kenneth, but to a man farther down on the social ladder of prominent area Jewish professionals, cantor Bobby Ornstein.

"Hook-nose, it's Lo Piccolo."

"Yup."

"I want you to lay off that thing over at Giuseppe Basi."

"No stink bombs tossed into the kitchen."

"Nope."

"No tires slashed in the parking lot."

"Nope. Nothing."

"I still get paid, you camel jockey."

"Your day rate still applies."

"Good. 'Cause Sensabaugh left me a message. He wants me to come in and talk about the Joe Bass beef."

"He's an assclown. He only made detective after he threatened to sue them over his wardrobe. He's a cross dresser."

"No shit. Why no more fun?"

"I think I may have figured out another way to stick it to that twat, Babe La Bruna. That restaurant will be mine in six months."

He clicked off and put in a call to the second Weinstein brother, Morris.

"Yeah, Morrie," Lo Piccolo said. "Put a stop payment on that bank check to Joe Bass Enterprises, Inc."

Eleven

The video production crew for *The Buck Stopped Here* arrived on schedule slightly after Frank Bruno had keyed open the restaurant to begin another sixteen-hour day. He was in a foul mood, exhausted, and he had completely forgotten to give Cousin Leonard the heads up on the crew's arrival.

"I can't be on the television. I can't be photographed," Cousin Leonard said, exasperated. "Nobody knows I work here except youse guys, on 'count of my accident."

Frank had only but to smile at the recent turn of events of his jumbled life. He had agreed to participate in Hayden Buckingham's television project not because she sexted him repeatedly. He did so in spite of the sexting. Nothing alarmed Frank more than apparent instability or unorthodoxy—especially in matters of sex—and his own vicissitudes had led him to place a premium on the appearance of normalcy.

No after careful deliberation, he decided to proceed with the show realizing that in doing so he was completely cutting off any possibility of a return to his former employer. Reality television was just about the quickest and most lethal way he could cement himself as *persona non grata* at the CIA

There were other considerations as well, he supposed.

He was fucking Babe La Bruna. She was fucking him. Anywhere and everywhere in the restaurant. The staff knew it, too, or at least they had sensed it, and they were talking.

Babe hired only beautiful women to work in the front of her house. Her hiring practices were deceptively simple; she could teach a server all that was required to perform in the manner expected of a restaurant with the reputation of Restaurant Giuseppe Basi. She could scrutinize their performance night after night, weeding out slowness and incompetence, but she could not fix a butterface—a candidate whose qualifications, attitude, and instincts matched everything befitting of a server of the highest standards…but her face.

The butterfaces made it to secondary tippable positions—hostess, busgirl, food runner; some even fell so far as to the coat checkroom and never progressed further.

The entire premise of a smooth-running, fire-on-all cylinders restaurant operation depended on the prospects of a significant amount of copulation between the front and back of house, and to a lesser extent between the front of the house and a segment of the clientele, otherwise known as the high-spending regulars (since the genetic talent pool of the back of the house at Restaurant Giuseppe Basi was severely limited, Babe wisely ratcheted up the eye candy in the front of house to ensure the regulars had a bevy of babes to ogle over on a nightly basis).

Babe knew that food and sex were the most powerful descriptors present at a highly successful restaurant. The only other descriptor to trump food and sex was fear and Restaurant Giuseppe Basi, until now, had seemed like a very safe place.

And here was Frank—worried about revealing Cousin Leonard's identity in order to spare him a reprisal from the Social Security administration and the state welfare office—instead of his own moral turpitude. If he thought his former job carried the heavy burden of such a judgment, it was clear he was unprepared for the choices he would face by re-entering the restaurant business.

The only thing Frank knew for certain when she appeared in a tight skirt and sweater was that he would like to choke out the slender neck from which Hayden Buckingham's faux reading glasses were suspended after this video business was all over.

"Frank, so wonderful to see you again. I'm so excited you and Babe agreed to do this."

"I've been seeing a lot of you lately."

"Very funny, Frank. You got my messages. You never texted back. Are you as shy as Babe says you are?"

"I'm very shy."

"Is Babe here? Can we start?"

"She's here. She's waiting for us downstairs in the office."

"Splendid," Hayden said, then turned to her crew. "How much longer before we're lit? We've got three days to get this all shot. Long days fellas, lots of overtime."

"Another twenty minutes, Ms. Buckingham."

"Let's adjourn below to the offices of Barbara La Bruna shall we? You've seen the script and the treatment."

"I have," Frank said.

"Wonderful. We'll be shooting B-Roll for most of today. Then we'll take actual scenes tomorrow and the next and then wrap."

"I have some questions."

"Save them, my dear, for the mysterious chambers of the woman of the house. All your questions will be answered."

Hayden and Babe greeted each other euro-style, three alternating kisses to the cheeks, then a long regard at arm's distance.

"We have some questions before we start," Babe said.

"Of course you do."

"Frank, do you want to start?"

"OK. Hayden, there's things written into the script here that we don't do at the restaurant."

"Such as?"

"Well, molecular gastronomy, *sous vide* to start."

"Let's take the sous vide first."

"What is sous vide?" Babe asked.

"It's a fancy term for immersing food in water in a plastic bag and letting it cook slowly," Frank said. "We don't do any of that here."

"Alright, here's the premise," Hayden said. "Kitchen Aid is a sponsor. They're coming out with a line of home sous vide equipment. When we brought them this show, they wanted in because their last experience with Joe's *Disaster Area* was incredible. They had record sales for his pasta extruder attachment on their mixers. I thought you could do the osso buco dish sous vide. It's a dish every little Italian-American housewife would like to produce but doesn't have the time. The crock pot just doesn't cut it anymore. This is the next generation crockpot—the KitchenAid Sous Vide."

"Alright. What about the molecular gastronomy scene?"

"Frank, it's all part of the back story. You are a CIA-trained chef. You've come in here after a terrible tragedy to help save the place. You're bringing the kitchen up to speed on modern techniques and trends. Babe is skeptical. It's part of the tension between you. That, and, of course, the sexual tension, and Joe's murder."

"I'm not comfortable with this."

"Then it's out. I want you to be comfortable."

"What about the part here where it says I started a program to recycle the restaurant's fryer oil and now use it to power my bio-diesel Toyota corolla?"

They all burst out laughing.

"Brilliant product placement isn't it?" Hayden Buckingham said with a twinkle. "When I brought the idea to Toyota, they went bonkers. Do you know how much brand erosion they've suffered with females thirty-and-up because they think that if they buy a Toyota their brakes are going to stick, and they'll shoot through the window of a storefront at their favorite strip plaza?"

"But the car…"

"It's out back, Frank. You didn't see. It's wonderful. Questions; please, more questions," Hayden said, and touched Babe's thigh.

"Alright, let's keep rolling. You say here that I decided to source all of my food locally from within a hundred miles of the restaurant."

"Ah, the sustainability play. That was a tough one to conceptualize but I think we found a way to do it."

"Let's hear it."

"OK. We all know what an absurd premise this locally raised movement is, right? Have you ever eaten at a place that really, truly sources their products locally? Dreadful. In the northeast, you've got chefs putting apiaries on the roofs of their restaurants to make honey. You have menus being written with the names of farms where—allegedly—the food comes from. And then you have the food itself. I don't need to tell you that a chef from Hoboken hanging his locally raised pig leg from the rafters of his restaurant's basement does not a prosciutto di Parma make."

"Agreed. So how are you going to pull this off?"

"Well for the vegetables, we're going to cut to a

greenhouse with plants and vines all over the place. The back story here is you struck a deal with a hydroponic tomato grower to grow ALL of your produce. He was reluctant at first but then he gave it a shot and IT'S WORKING."

"Who's 'he?'"

"He is an actor. They're all actors, except you, Babe, the Detective, what's his name?"

"Sensabaugh."

"Yes remind me to talk to him today. He's talking some wild shit about me doing another pilot. Something about the secret lives of law enforcement officials and crossdressers. There's a couple more."

"Who else?" Babe asked.

"Well, there's the first woman to appear on Joe's *Disaster Area* show. She gives a real tearful testimonial about him."

"That putana from Westchester? Her husband caught her giving Joe a hand job at their holiday party. They live in Chappaqua, two blocks away from the Clintons. As a matter of fact, Joe said they were at the party and Bill Clinton hit on her too but she shut him down"

"Babe, you are so clinical about your dead husband," Hayden said.

"Habit," Babe replied. "I have a couple of my own questions. In scene two, you have me walking through a cemetery. I throw a rose at Joe's gravesite. Joe doesn't have a gravesite. He's upstairs behind the bar."

"Babe this is television. We have reverse angles. You don't see the actual name on the tombstone."

"Moving along. You have here that the restaurant has reopened but business is slow."

"Yes."

"We've been mobbed ever since we've reopened."

"Again, we need back stories. Here it is kids—a tragic death occurred. One of America's most beloved chefs—albeit for a certain segment of the population—was murdered right in his own restaurant. Who did it? Theories will be posited. We're considering a phone poll. How will the restaurant survive? How will the family rally together in the face of great tragedy and move toward closure? You don't serve lunch, right Babe?"

"Right."

"Bingo. So that's our slow restaurant. Do you see where I'm going with this?"

"I like it. I've liked it ever since you first showed it to me. Frank was not on board. I've convinced him. We just had some last-minute questions."

Hayden's production assistant, Rafale Deschamps, walked in with a clay pot of steaming yerba maté tea and set it on a linen napkin with three cups.

"We are lit, Ms. Buckingham," he said.

"Did you hear that?" Hayden Buckingham said. "We are lit. There's no turning back now. Are you ready, Frank? Are you ready to be videotaped?"

"Against my better judgment, yes."

"You're still sticking around after this is over to be a judge in the *Sauce Off,*" Babe said. "That was the deal."

"Babe, this show is going to be seen by millions. It's

seven figures worth of exposure for the restaurant. You'll have every tour operator from Japan to Buenos Aires booking with you when this gets into syndication. And you're worried about a local-yokel sauce competition."

"Yes, I am," Babe said. "We have a lot of enemies around here. Nobody wants us to win. They want us to lose. I hear what you are saying about the show and all but this is Niagara Falls and none of that matters. I promised the organizing committee that you would be a judge and they went apeshit."

"I'll be there Babe," Hayden smiled.

Babe was right. Everything in the restaurant business mattered. She also did a dead-on impersonation while pouring out the yerba maté: "I'm Hayden Buckingham. *The Buck Stopped Here."*

TWELVE

Boned: The Life and Death of Chef Joe Bass

Fade in to: Exterior of Terrapin Point at Niagara Falls.

It's a bitter winter day at the Falls. Ice covers the trees from the spewing mist, encasing everything into a giant snow globe. In the distance, seagulls take flight against the barren blue sky.

The dramatic figure of raven-haired Babe La Bruna dressed in a long winter coat, scarf, and boots appears at the rail overlooking the Falls. She ponders the water. It is mesmerizing and soothing to her troubled soul.

Hayden Buckingham (HB) Voice Over

Nobody could have foreseen the turn of events for one of America's most recognizable chefs. These events have haunted Barbara La Bruna for the past six months, turned her world upside-down, inside-out. After years of struggling, scraping, and surviving in the brutally tough restaurant busi-

ness, her husband was discovered. He became a star on the Food Network. He was colorful, controversial; he spoke his mind and that's why America loved him. He gave a voice to the voiceless in the world of food. He spoke simply and from the heart. And people remembered what he said, especially when he delivered his trademark phrase:

Cut to scene from *Disaster Area*

This meal is a Disaster Area....

HB—Yes, Chef Joe Bass had declared a Disaster Area on many home cooks but he did it in such a way as to endear him to the hearts of us all.

Cut to Westchester Housewife (WH) testimonial

WH—I'll never forget that first episode. I was so nervous. I had never been on TV before and then there I was, on the Food Network. I met Rachel Ray, Tyler Florence, Paula Deen, but when Joe Bass walked into the room, he owned it. My Swedish meatballs—my Grandmum's trademark recipe—was the first dish ever that Chef Joe Bass declared a Disaster Area. Now that's a bit of Chef Joe Bass trivia for you.

Cut to Babe La Bruna in same winter apparel walking through St. Joseph's cemetery. She has a rose in her hand. She makes the sign of the cross at a grave and then releases the rose in her hand to the ground. It lands on the fresh snow, like blood spilling out of body onto a clean floor.

HB—These were heady times for Chef Joe Bass and his wife Babe La Bruna. Chef was making a hefty salary outside the restaurant and Babe was keeping the restaurant—booked to capacity—humming along. But all of that would be turned upside down in a single moment.

Cut to Interview with Detective Nathan Sensabaugh

(NS). While the detective is giving us his narration we see a quick sequence of CSI-type generic shots of a crime scene, et cetera.

NS—When we arrived at the restaurant that morning, officers observed Mrs. La Bruna kneeling over her husband who had been stabbed. She was applying pressure to his wound. He had bled profusely. He was pronounced dead upon arrival at Niagara Falls Memorial Hospital, one Giuseppe Basi of 462 Fourth Street, Niagara Falls, NY. The deceased was forty-four years old. The coroner ruled his death a homicide by an acute puncture of his chest cavity resulting in Class III catastrophic hemorrhage. No suspects have been arrested or charged yet.

Cut to slow motion footage of Chef Joe Bass from *Disaster Area,* then cut back to Babe at the brink of the Falls.

HB—Suddenly, one of America's favorite culinary voices was silenced. And how do you carry on when the name of your restaurant is inextricably linked to a man who had declared his last Disaster Area?

Cut to Babe La Bruna (BLB), interior of an empty restaurant.

BLB—I was in shock for weeks after Joe's death. The support from the community was overwhelming and comforting. I just couldn't believe he was gone. Nobody could. After things quieted down that's when I had the most trouble. I didn't know what to do. I had spent the last twelve years working in the restaurant every day and night. Then it's all taken away from you. I wanted to close down, sell the place, and just move away....

Cut to exterior of Hayden Buckingham walking up to the front entrance of the restaurant.

HB—But Babe La Bruna did not close down. She had

the help of her family and her husband's extended family. They all pitched in at the crucial moment, none more so that one individual who was not related Chef Joe Bass but nevertheless called him his brother.

Cut to interior of kitchen. Frank Bruno (FB) is Cryovacing veal shanks and inserting them into a KitchenAid sous vide machine.

HB—His name is Frank Bruno. He is a Culinary Institute of America graduate and has cooked overseas for foreign dignitaries and at American embassies the world over. He was also Chef Joe Bass's closest friend. They grew up together in a home just a stone's throw from the restaurant. In their early years they were inseparable. Each pursued a career in the culinary arts—Chef Joe at the local community college and Chef Frank at the prestigious Culinary Institute of America. They drifted apart as is normal with age, but when Chef Joe was murdered, Frank Bruno came home. He wanted to help out.

Cut to close up of Frank Bruno in chef's whites. He's thoughtful; pensive but with a smoldering intensity.

FB—In all the tragedy, I didn't want Babe to lose the restaurant as well. I thought that after things settled down, we could re-open for a while. I would help her in the kitchen. I had the time to spare. I didn't want her to make a rash decision and just walk away from everything.

Cut to Hayden Buckingham approaching the restaurant front entrance.

HB—But if Restaurant Giuseppe Basi was to survive and prosper, Chef Frank Bruno knew some things had to change. The menu, for example; it had not had a makeover in nearly a decade. Chef Bruno wanted to implement some minor tweaks and update and add some dishes. Babe La Bruna was skeptical. She didn't know if change would help carry the restaurant forward.

Cut to interior of a hydroponic greenhouse. We see various shots of vegetable plants growing through the silhouette of a dramatic winter land-scape. It's a *Wizard of Oz* landscape of vegetation. Frank appears in street clothes and talks to the plant manager. The plant manager (PM) has a clipboard. He's taking Frank's order.

PM—When Chef Bruno approached me about growing the restaurant's produce locally, all here at the facility, I just didn't think it could be done. But he convinced me to give it a try. He knew of others that had been doing it for years; people in the Scandinavian countries who grew their in-ventory year round in facilities like this. He made a compelling case that this was the future of the food business.

Cut to close up of Frank on site at the green-house examining plants. He's now wearing a lab coat and safety glasses.

FB—I knew that once we had a great head of ice-berg lettuce, everything else would fall into place. It's the little things that matter. In a couple months we will have our entire inventory sourced locally. We've set up a partnership with a slaughterhouse in the Southern Tier to humanely slaughter our proteins. We will have computerized records and certifications of herd, species and lineage. At some point we'll be able to bring you a JPEG image of the animal you are about to con-sume right at your table on an iPad. That picture will verify to you that the animal had no fear and was relaxed before it was slaughtered, so that there can be no concern as to any cortisol release coursing through the animal's system pri-or to death.

Cut to Frank in the Toyota biodiesel. We see a deep fryer being drained of spent oil, put into containers, then Frank pouring it into the gas take of the car.

FB—I wanted the restaurant to think about sustainability in different ways. It was not just a matter of would we survive without Joe, but how could we reuse and recycle the materials we use on daily basis to cut our carbon footprint. Everything was on the table for discussion.

Cut to Hayden in the restaurant parking lot. Frank is unloading his cases of product for the restaurant from his crammed car.

HB—Every morning, Chef Bruno wakes up before dawn and races off to source his locally grown vegetables and humanely slaughtered meats and he does so on the oil that was in his deep fryer the night before.

Cut to Frank Bruno driving along the highway. He's conversational, reflective…

FB—When I get past fifty-five, that's when you can really smell the calamari. We don't fry a whole lot, but we reserve one fryer exclusively for the calamari. Can you smell it? I can always tell if the kitchen is coating the calamari correctly. We use a simple flour and crushed red pepper breading. We don't do anything fancy like soak the calamari in milk before, or use corn starch or corn meal. If I can smell the red pepper in the Toyota, I know they are doing things right at the fry station.

Cut to interior of empty restaurant. There's no one there.

HB—But change has its price. Perhaps because of the violent end that Chef Joe Bass met, or perhaps the general sentiment that things could never be the same without him, the restaurant re-

mained quiet for the first months after it reopened... No progress was made in the murder investigation... Babe La Bruna was having second thoughts... and Frank Bruno was pushing the envelope in the kitchen, challenging his crew to go even further on the razor's edge. But all of that was about to change. Join us next time for *Boned: The Life and Death of Chef Joe Bass.*

Wrap

It was a twelve-hour day of shooting on top of another full shift at night in the kitchen. The restaurant was slammed again—one hundred fifty covers on a Tuesday night. Frank dragged himself to the bar and asked barkeep Jimmy Cruickshank to pour him a triple of Maker's Mark. He drank in silence then managed to fumble his way to the car. The smell of spent fryer oil in the Toyota nearly gagged him. He stank of the kitchen, of food cooked that had embedded itself into his skin. His forearm had been burned from a grease splash at the sauté station and his feet were throbbing.

When he entered his apartment, wanting only to shower his foul body, he was greeted by the sight of Hayden Buckingham and Babe La Bruna on his couch, freshly showered, drinking wine and smoking a joint.

"Hi Frank," Babe said, "we've been waiting patiently for you."

"Not so patiently," Hayden smirked.

"You've got to be kidding me; I'm exhausted."

He fell immediately to sleep.

If he dreamed that night, Frank could not remember. It could not have been any worse than what his life, in the restaurant business, had become.

Thirteen

The twenty-third Annual *Sauce Off* to benefit the Greater Niagara American Cancer Society was a sold-out affair. With the participation of Restaurant Giuseppe Basi and the presence of celebrity judge Hayden Buckingham, all tickets sold within ten minutes of posting on line. The local furrier, Feldman's Furs, had to put on an extra shift to retrieve mink coats out of cold storage for such a momentous occasion for all the "Ladies Who Lunch" that gobbled up the tickets.

There hadn't been this much fur on the floor of the Seneca Casino since the facility, formerly known as the Niagara Falls Convention Center, hosted Frank Sinatra's one and only area appearance In the Round.

The only other time—beside the Chairman of the-Board's final appearance in 1977—that locals could recall such a spectacle of fur, pearls, fake diamonds, and Cadillacs idling in the valet line was during the dreadful Trans-Siberian Orchestra concert outing that took place annually over the holidays.

You might think a person of Hayden Buckingham's stature in the food community might thumb her perfectly sculpted nose at an event such as the *Sauce Off.*

You would be incorrect.

Buckingham relished these cheesy affairs, in the way a highly regarded chef devours a bag of overly salted potato chips or Doritos in the privacy of his or her own lair. As long as you met Buckingham's appearance fee—typically 5 to 10 K depending on length of stay—she was there from the start, stayed late to sign autographs, and she performed like a true champ.

On this occasion, however, she had waived her fee in deference to Babe La Bruna, and in doing so was treated as visiting royalty by the local organizing committee, comprised mostly of senior members of the Red Hat Society and the Junior League of Women.

And why shouldn't Hayden Buckingham be stoked to judge the best marinara sauce on the Niagara Frontier in front of a packed house at the Seneca Niagara Casino? Never mind the fact that Clint Holmes was the musical entertainment for the affair, and that she had carried a weird crush on the lounge lizard ever since she was a child and first saw him appear on the Jerry Lewis Muscular Dystrophy telethon. Her love of "Jerry's Kids" was one possible explanation for her fetishistic appreciation of these over-the-top communal events.

The other explanation for her jubilant mood could be that she had just wrapped *Boned: The Life and Death of Chef Joe Bass* and the Discovery Channel, after previewing the dailies, had ordered six more episodes.

Fade In—Hayden Buckingham walking down the steps from the front entrance of Restaurant Giuseppe Basi. It's a late winter evening; snow is falling. The restaurant is illuminated but the daylight slowly fading.

HB—So, six months after the fact, the murder of Chef Joe Bass remains unsolved. Detective Nathan Sensabaugh says the Niagara Falls Police Department is pursuing multiple theories but they are lacking that one pivotal clue that would help them break the case. DNA collected at the scene points in multiple directions. And in the balance lies the fate of a family, a restaurant, and a city. This is Hayden Buckingham... *The Buck Stopped Here.*

Fade out

Up until five years ago, the *Sauce Off* was a predetermined competition. The invitees would rotate top honors on a yearly basis and retain all rights to advertise in the *Niagara Gazette* in the coveted Dine Out section as "Voted Niagara's Best Sauce" without threat of litigation or retaliation.

Each of the top five houses of red sauce displayed an identical plaque in the foyer of their restaurant. Only the year and a few minor ingredient disclaimers on the plaque needed to be changed to distinguish each year's winning sauce.

For example, in 1988, Stormin' Norman's took first place for their Ragù alla Cacciatore that featured the famous Panepinto house-made garlic sausages devoid of any cheese or fennel seeds in the mix. In 1999, Da Alfredo won for Salsa di Marche, served as the accompaniment to their Lasagna Marche, an ode to Alfredo Cuneo's roots in Ancona.

Even in the early days of Restaurant Giuseppe Basi, Chef Joe hesitated to participate in the *Sauce Off* on the principle that it was not a true competition. When he became famous, he refused to participate on the basis that he had everything to lose and nothing to gain—he didn't want anyone to brag that they had 'beaten' Chef Joe Bass and his famous Salsa di Pomodoro.

But when he agreed to be a celebrity judge one year—declaring Neddy's House of Spaghetti's Salsa ai Pieducci a Disaster Area—he was vilified and banned from the premises by all the other houses of red sauce and told to never come back, not even as a spectator.

"That's no hair off my balls," Chef Joe told the incensed gathering of restaurant owners, especially Nelson Tabone of Neddy's House of Spaghetti, who vowed to slit his throat.

But fearing the event had lost its luster, and more importantly, eager to sate the public desire to see a wobbly-produced facsimile of the Food Network's *Iron Chef*, the *Sauce Off* committee decided to go legit and throw caution and hurt feelings to the wind.

Suddenly, the Sauce Off meant something.

The rules had changed and nobody as of yet had figured out a way to game the system until Babe La Bruna threw her stockpot into the ring with chief judge Hayden Buckingham tucked into the confines of her Seven Jeans for all Mankind's back pocket.

The rules were as follows—you could not bring anything cooked into the competition kitchen, which was located off stage in the casino's foodservice commissary. Each team was comprised of two members. All goods had to be checked through by Seneca security personnel who had agreed to perform the careful screening of ingredients and certification of their pristine state.

In a scene of reverse discrimination—finally, the Red Man was patting down the White Man—multiple-times participants had been barred from the competition after cooked precursors to their sauce had been smuggled into the kitchen, only to be discovered by the security team.

All teams were assigned a 40-quart stockpot in which to produce the sauce. There would be no more than six hours allotted to the sauce production. Each sauce would be served in an identical white china monkey dish and any herb garnishment was expressly forbidden. The committee wanted to see red sauce and only red sauce in those monkey dishes. If the sauce was a ragù, then the protein added to it had to be strained from the final sample so as to not exceed what was commonly accepted as a smooth viscosity.

Norman Panepinto's Ragù alla Cacciatore had lost

last year for his failure to heed this one important prerequisite straining procedure. Judges were to use soup spoons and the crusts of bread to sample the sauce.

Frank greeted the *Sauce Off* and the prospect of working on a Sunday—the kitchen's only day of rest—with the disdain and indignity of a veteran restaurant professional. His kitchen crew, an assembly of newly-minted community college culinary grads, Pops De Simone, and, of course, Cousin Leonard, was collectively exhausted and had not had a moment to look up from their re-opening. They were doing a record amount of covers for the off-season and the Saturday night prior to the *Sauce Off* had wiped out their entire stock of prepped inventory. Frank told them to stay home and rest up. He would handle this 'thing' himself. Deep down, Frank saw the wisdom of Joe Bass's reluctance to participate—everything to lose and nothing to gain—and this Sunday distraction seemed like more work for the weary.

Babe did not see things that way.

She and Frank locked horns when she found out he was planning to serve their salsa di pomodoro with cappellini instead of the house ragù with rigatoni.

"The pomodoro is totally inappropriate for this thing," she told Frank. "It's not even a sauce. It's reduced plum tomatoes, basil, salt, and olive oil."

"Precisely. It won't take long. I'm spent, Babe. The kitchen is exhausted. We do not need to do this, but if you think it's important, I'll go along with it to a point. The point ends at salsa di pomodoro."

Babe restrained her impulse for a rebuttal. The deafening silence between them on this one point illustrated the centuries-old tension between front of the house and back of the house.

What is more important to a restaurant, good food or good service?

Somehow, the good food side of the conundrum has taken precedence over the service part of the equation in our perception of restaurant reality. It is an evolutionary error much in the same way Richard Dawkins attributed our belief in the Almighty as an evolutionary delusion. But unlike Dawkins and his group of bomb throwers, this was not an argument that has a way forward.

It was also an argument that Babe realized she could not prevail in unless she was willing to cook the ragù herself, and that was something she was not about to do, not in her newly purchased Seven Jeans for All Mankind *(three hundred dollars for a pair of jeans. Joe would have flipped).*

"The pomodoro is too sublime. Do you think this mass of flesh will appreciate it?" she asked, in an astute attempt at front-of-the-house logic to sway Frank in her direction, when a more direct approach—perhaps an unshowered body, unwashed hair and a robe concealing nothing more than a pair of chocolate brown cheekies—would have been more effective.

"That's not for us to reason why," Frank said. "This *Sauce Off* means nothing. I can't believe it matters to you."

"It does."

"Why is that?"

"Because it's what my family will talk about ad infinitum. For years they've wanted Joe and me to do this. It sounds corny; I know. But so was the Homecoming Dance. So is my wedding album. So was Joe's Camaro. So are your desert boots, Frank."

"This is about you not becoming Homecoming Queen? Who was our Homecoming Queen?"

"Maria Bongiovanni," Babe said without hesitation. "Have you seen her Facebook photo? She's as big as a house."

"Good Lord."

"I understand everything about the pomodoro. Joe lectured me about it all the time."

"No, you don't. Do you see these cans of tomatoes stripped of their labels? They were shipped from a food broker's warehouse in Salerno. I met this man personally. I set up this relationship for Joe, and I bought the first container's worth of inventory to get him started."

"I know. They are the real San Marzano tomatoes."

"No they are not. You see, San Marzano tomatoes do not exist anymore. When Joe first came to me ten years ago he was adamant: 'I need San Marzanos. You need me to find San Marzanos.' So I located this broker in Salerno and said, 'Look, I need San Marzanos and we'll buy a container of them to start.' He said he was willing to take my money but that San Marzanos do not exist anymore. The plant species is extinct. He said the Italian government had covered up this fact with an elaborate ruse and went to so far as to set up a phony certification process so they could falsify the authenticity of the tomatoes they planned to sell abroad."

"Can you spare me the back story? I've heard it a million times."

"Then let me repeat it so there is no misunderstanding. So the broker says to me, 'I have tomatoes that are better than the phony San Marzanos.' He said he could sell me canned tomatoes from a single estate farm outside of Corbara, a small town in the hills of Campania. The highly prize Pomodorini di Corbara, completely unknown outside of Italy. Fine. I had a contact do the paperwork. And from that moment forward, we've been buying all of the tomatoes for this restaurant from this one food broker. They are shipped into New York and labeled and housed in Long Island. Then they are stripped of their labels and shipped directly here. There is no distributor. No middleman. Nobody outside of Joe and I know where they come from. And that's why we have the salsa di pomodoro."

"Because of tomatoes from Corbara."

"Not exactly. I checked up on the food broker a couple years ago. He had stopped shipping us the highly prized Pomodorino di Corbara. The farm he was getting them from went out of business, so he just substituted another variety and continued shipping to us. Four times a year."

"Did you ever tell Joe this?"

"What we were getting from this guy was so superior to what else was on the market that I didn't have the heart. Then Joe publicly made a big stink in front of Mario Batali about how his San Marzano tomatoes were a Disaster Area and a fraud and it was one of his most highly-rated shows."

"Why did Joe do that? I could never understand why he cut off his nose to spite his face with the other chefs at the Food Network."

"Recognition. Deep down inside Joe thought his moment in the spotlight would end soon enough and that he was just a *mameluke* from Niagara Falls. You see, Frank, we all want recognition, don't we? Even if it must be metered out at a *Sauce Off.*"

By the time Frank arrived at the casino for the *Sauce Off* and cleared security, he was already in a decidedly better mood. He immediately recognized the Seneca security guard checking his ingredients and he knew the names and faces of all of his competitors. It was like scrolling through an updated version of his high school year book; an un-Photoshopped version of the terrible reality of facial aging, and the unrestrained growth of facial hair, most commonly referred to in the popular literature as the mustache.

The men wearing chef's coats who had remained in town and in the restaurant business all looked equally terrible. And they all smoked cigarettes which, strangely enough, was permitted in the kitchen area of the casino since it was not technically a part of the United States anymore but was in the domain of the sovereign Seneca Nation of Indians and therefore not subject to any local, state, or federal regulations regarding the sanitary operations of foodservice.

"Hey Frankie," Bubba O'Donnell, the sous chef from Da Alfredo, said, "I heard you was in town and cooking at Joe's place."

"Nice to see you again, Bubba. Staying out of trouble?"

"Been sober now six years."

"What about Miles Away? He still cooking for Norman?"

"Oh yeah. He'll never leave. They'll have to scrape him off the kitchen floor like they did Joe to get him out of that place."

Larry "Miles Away" Rubino was so-named by local law enforcement officials after this youthful scofflaw had a permanent buttress for an alibi—his mother, Roxie Rubino—who insisted that little Larry was "Miles Away" from the scene of the crime.

"Hey, chooch," Miles Away came up behind Frank, "did I hear my name spoken?"

"How's your mother?" Frank said warmly.

"Passed on over fifteen years ago. You wouldn't have known that. You been away Frank."

"Miles away," Frank replied and they hugged each other.

"Whoa, it's *finocchio?* I can't believe he showed up. Where's Babe? Where's the grand *baccalà?*"

"Hello, Bebe," Frank said.

"Well, if it isn't the local president of the NAACP," Miles Away said.

"Shut up, Larry. Before I put you through that window."

"Not unless I do it first," Chef Harold Gildersleeve "Bobo" Watson said with a giant grin. "How are you doing, Frank? Miles. Bubba. You white trash boys ready to take second place and an ass-whipping today at the *Sauce Off?*"

"Bobo, remember the time we were in gym class—actually in the shower after gym class," Miles Away said. "And Mickey Sweeney started busting your balls about how black guys don't like to eat pussy and you turned on us with that crowbar dong and said, 'When you got the pole, you don't eat the hole.'"

"I still got the pole, limp dick. You just can't get the image of me in the shower out of your head. You're the real finocchio here," Bobo said. "Now give me a cigarette. And not those filthy Indian cigarettes they sell here; I want certified Brown and Williamson product."

When the final cigarettes had been smoked and stamped out in the parking lot, the competitors all filed back into the kitchen of the casino. It could have been a pick-up game of basketball at the YMCA or a game of shinny at the local ice pavilion. Soon, they would be keeping score for keeps. This was a competition.

May the best sauce win.

"Feed the masses, sleep with the classes. Isn't that what your father used to say, Lo Piccolo?" Miles Away shouted over the kitchen commotion. "Isn't that how he ended up putting all that sugar in his sauce?"

The last competitor was none other than Nelson Tabone from Neddy's House of Spaghetti, who had cooked every meal that came out of his kitchen, just like his father had before him, and his father had before that. The House of Spaghetti company apron—complete with a cartoonish logo of spaghetti twirled over a fork—was tossed in Nelson's direction when his father Edward retired and all that had to be done was to swap out the *E* for an *Ne* in the House of Spaghetti's neon Channellock illuminated sign.

Nelson was a singularly bad cook but brilliantly so in the manner of all successful bad cooks since he cooked everything equally badly—meat, poultry, seafood, pasta—thus his restaurant was always busy—not slammed—but with a steady enough stream of business for those who appreciated bad cooking. Don't kid yourself. There are millions—not if tens of millions—of people that prefer bad cuisine.

Feed the masses, sleep with the classes.

"Let's see them, King George," Bubba O'Donnell said to Nelson Tabone. "Let's see those pig's trotters. Do you know Einstein's definition of insanity? It's not doing the same thing over and over and expecting a different result. It's putting pig's feet in your sauce and expecting to win the *Sauce Off.*"

Nelson Tabone suffered from an intractable speech

impediment—stammering, not stuttering—hence the reference to King George VI. His rebuttal to Bubba O'Donnell was so delayed that had it been closed captioned for video transcription, the transcriber could have completed Nelson Tabone's thoughts for him in a more expeditious manner.

"You are a filthy cook who shouldn't even be allowed in the kitchen."

The other thing about Nelson Tabone's linguistic impediment—perhaps unrelated to this phenomenon and, in fact, some would argue inversely proportional to it—was that nobody ever complained about the speed of the kitchen or the service at the House of Spaghetti. They were both lightning fast.

Frank had a game plan that he stuck to while the other chefs proceeded to crack open their number ten cans of plum tomatoes, took their boning knives to the wet Cryovaced carcasses of meat, and tied-off whatever *bouquet garni* was aimed for their stockpot. It was all a very macho scene in the beginning. In some ways it resembled that other great display of male testosterone, the a group of weightlifters in the warm up phase before a bench press competition.

Frank left his unmarked cans of Corbara tomatoes out on the prep table next to a bunch of fresh basil and an unmarked bleeker of olive oil. He started drinking a bottle of wine, completed it, then he switched to a cooler of beer at his side.

"It's really all that simple, huh, big shot?" Miles Away Rubino asked.

"It really is, Larry," Frank said. He had appropriated a swivel chair from one the chef's cubbyholes and was surveying the scene. "Do you want a beer?"

"Love one."

"What about you, Bobo?"

"In a minute, let me just get this set here and I'll join you. How's Pops?"

"He's not getting any better. He really misses you."

"He misses a ride to and from work. That's what he misses. And the scratch-off lottery tickets I'd buy him on payday. Stage two pancreatic cancer and he's scratching away like he has the rest of eternity."

"How's it going, King George?" Miles Away shouted.

Nelson Tabone was immersed in a sudoku book while his sauce simmered on the stove. He paid no attention to his competitors.

"I'm ready to take a steam," Frank said. "Anybody with me? They have this quasi-sweat lodge over at the casino hotel spa."

"I don't know about that, Frank," Bubba said. "Think we have enough time?"

"Gents, there's four hours before this debacle starts. That's plenty of time to get in a good sweat. They've even got some Cambodian boat chicks over there at the spa for rubdowns."

"Happy ending?" Miles Away said. "I'm in. Let's go, Mr. I-don't-eat-the-hole."

The towel snapping outside of the steam room was a sure sign that Frank' s plan was working. Within a few hours, Bobo had passed out from a mixture of heat, alcohol consumption, and hypertension; and Miles Away was slumped over a trash can vomiting the undigested remains of a cheese steak into a trash canister. Hotel security for the casino had to be summoned after Bubba terrified his unfortunately-chosen Cambodian masseuse. O'Donnell had demanded an encore of the highly anticipated happy ending without an additional charge and that did not wash well with the management of the sweat lodge.

But the real drama of the moment, and the entire *Sauce Off* in general, was actually occurring in a conference room a few floors below the hotel spa. That's where all the owners of the competing restaurants had gathered for the annual *Sauce Off* mixer featuring a copious amount of top-shelf liquor and passed both hors d'oeuvres and industry gossip.

The event was hosted, as usual, by Stormin' Norman Panepinto, the dean of red sauce and a man well into his seventies who was still not afraid to get his hands dirty in his namesake restaurant, rolling up the monogrammed sleeves of his poplar dress shirts and washing dishes in his dish pit.

Stormin' Norman looked forward to this event more than anything else on his calendar, even more than New Year's Eve, when his auxiliary dining room, the seldom used Stormin' Salon, was completely booked.

He always had a brand-new suit cut for the occasion by a traveling garment salesman from Hong Kong, who Stormin' Norman had done business with for thirty years. Chauncey Chin Chuman (CCC) of Hong Kong Tailors had never botched a Stormin' Norman Panepinto double-breasted summer wool suit with the unusual measurements of 42, 18.5, 55, 28.

"I'm so glad you could all make it here again," Stormin' Norman said. "Babe, we are especially delighted to have you with us this year, especially as we all share in your tragedy."

A complete moment of silence.

"Gentlemen," Stormin' Norman continued. "This is the *Sauce Off's* twenty-third year. We've raised millions of dollars for the American Cancer Society. What a blessed country and industry we all wake up to each and every morning. Is there anything better than the U.S. of A and the hospitality industry?"

Continued silence.

"We all know how difficult the last two years have been with the economy in the tank. Some of you cut prices to maintain volume and cash flow. I don't blame you. We never did because my accountant wouldn't let me. We were already at the bottom of the barrel. It was a scary time. People stopped going out to eat. A lot of the smaller guys closed shop. The rumors started. Even our name came up. Is Stormin' Norman going out? I heard the whispers. I looked at my dining room night after night—empty—and wondered myself, *is* Stormin' Norman going out?"

On cue a trio of servers appeared in the conference room carrying trays.

"We all know full well that things aren't what they used to be. The numbers don't lie. The only thing that lies is you, my fine colleagues in hospitality. You lie. And so do I. Business is great, right? No, business sucks. It sucks balls worse than at any time in my fifty years in this business.

"And to top it all off now our great state, the State of New York, wants to audit each and every one of our businesses. I'm sure you've all received your notices. I got mine from the Department of Labor last week. I got one for Weights and Measures, one for Unemployment, one for Worker's Compensation, and of course, the granddaddy of them all, one from State Sales Tax."

The servers spread out and positioned themselves at strategic points along the conference table.

"Our state is horribly broke and impossibly in debt. The one solution that our Governor and Senators and Assemblymen have come up with is to wring more dollars out of small businesses through aggressive audits. But I did not survive in this business for five decades without a little help along the way; a little providence and guidance from people in the right places; people who give me information about what is *really* going on."

Stormin' motioned to the servers to place a monkey dish of tomato sauce in front of each of the attendees.

"You know, in all the years I've attended this event I never sampled anyone else's sauce. I just didn't want to entertain the possibility that someone's sauce might be better than mine. If that was so, then how could I wake up the next morning, knowing that somebody had better sauce than Stormin' Norman? Do you agree, Bebe?"

Bebe Lo Piccolo readjusted his seat.

"I thought it might be a good idea if we all tasted each other's sauces this year before they went to the judge's table, since this is a level playing field now. It's what they call the Age of Transparency. That's why I toast all of you now, not with a glass of champagne, but with the one product that has helped us to endure the greatest economic turmoil since the Great Depression—our sauce. Drink up!"

Stormin' Norman was standing over Bebe Lo Piccolo.

Alfredo Cuneo, Pietro Prato, Babe La Bruna, and Nelson Tabone all looked at each other. Had the old man finally gone nuts?

"Go on, Bebe, drink your sauce."

"Norman what kind of bullshit is this? Is this some kind of karaoke re-enactment of Al Capone? Have your meds been regulated or what the fuck?"

Stormin' Norman put the barrel of a 45 revolver next to Bebe Lo Piccolo's head.

"Drink up," he said.

"You know I'm allergic to tomatoes."

"Drink up, you little sniveling canary. You think you can cut a deal with the State Tax authority and Stormin' Norman won't know about it?"

Bebe Lo Piccolo began to sweat.

"If I drink that I'll blow up like a balloon. My windpipe will close in less than a minute."

"And if you don't drink it, I'll blow your head straight off."

Bebe Lo Piccolo looked down at the monkey dish set before him. He consumed less than an ounce of tomato sauce, most of which spouted out the sides of his mouth and down his trembling cheeks. Sure enough, his face turned red and he stared panting for air. He ripped his tie and suit coat off.

He was in a complete anaphylaxis within a minute. That's when Stormin' Norman pulled a hypodermic needle from his newly cut Hong Kong tailored suit and plunged 0.5 ml of adrenaline into Lo Piccolo's neck.

"And the winner of the *2010 Greater Niagara American Cancer Society Sauce Off* is," Hayden Buckingham stood at the microphone on the dais, waiting for the envelope," Neddy's House of Spaghetti, owned by Nelson Tabone!"

An ecstatic and flabbergasted Nelson Tabone rushed the stage. Hayden kissed him on both cheeks then fully on the lips. The audience roared. Frank, who was legally intoxicated and standing next to Babe, began whistling and cheering as if he were at a rock concert.

The fact of the matter was that Nelson Tabone's Ragù ai Pieducci was the only sauce that had made it to the judge's table that afternoon. Given the general chaos behind the scenes, the organizing committee quickly arrived at the prudent decision to use Tabone's sauce as a default prop in all the monkey dishes sent for public judging. Hayden Buckingham proved her mettle when describing the winning entry.

"You are right on trend today, Nelson. And you might not even realize it. I've seen chefs all over the country use the pig in many creative ways. They host snout-to-tail parties in their restaurants and collaborate with each other on ways to use the entire animal, breaking it down to its very essence, harvesting all the goodness of the sow. Your sauce is in that league.'

The definitive final comments of the evening belonged to Nelson Tabone. His speech was decades in the making and almost as long in its delivery.

"When my . . . grandfather . . . wanted to open a restaurant . . . he was told where he could . . . open. . . . He was given the . . . worst possible location . . . the sticks. . . . But he never complained. . . . He embraced the community. He . . . made friends with the Amish, . . . the Mennonites, the Quakers, . . . the rednecks; . . . they brought him all sorts of things . . . including the feet off their pigs. . . . which they . . . might have thrown out after . . . slaughter, . . . had it not been for my grandfather . . . who told bring them to him . . . so he could make sauce. . . . Thank you."

FOURTEEN

Frank received a startling email from the personal email account of Marvin P. Reed, Ambassador of the United States of America to the Italian Republic. The email had actually been kicked to a spam folder and retrieved by mere coincidence. It was two weeks old but Frank decided to open it. He read it, pondered, and then decided to reply.

The response to his reply was almost immediate:

"Where have you been? I need to meet with you here. Request of CUC. Call me at this number…"

Frank dialed the number and was immediately connected to the Ambassador.

"Bruno, it has been almost impossible to get a hold of you! My requests to your former employer have been ignored."

"How did you find me?"

"Believe it or not, I got so damn frustrated I Googled

you one day. And I got this crazy result from YouTube—some cooking show or something like that from the Discovery Channel—*Boned,* or something."

"I guess that seals it; I really am out of the business."

"Bruno, I need you to come to Rome. Cardinal Craxi has been pressing for a meeting with you. He really wants to meet with you. No intermediaries. I don't know what he wants to discuss. We have been familiar for a long time and despite your opinion of him, it's rather more complicated than that. Can you come?"

"Where is the meeting?" Frank asked.

"A place has not been chosen yet. It can't be at the Vatican or the Embassy."

"I think I know a place."

"Does that mean you'll come?"

"If we can do it at Piazza Sallustio at the Hotel Londra, day after tomorrow, and I can be back by Friday. I'm a working man now. I've got a fully-booked dining room for Friday and Saturday night."

"What—?"

A car was waiting for Frank outside the Fiumicino Airport. He agreed to the meeting more out of a palpable desire to escape the seemingly inescapable rigors of kitchen work than whatever the nefarious Cardinal Umberto Craxi might have sought from him. That was a different life. A different time.

Babe was not pleased with Frank's decision but was

marginally assuaged by his assurances that the new kitchen crew could handle the load. He had never intended to become the new head chef in Joe Bass's absence nor—may the Lord forgive his transgression—the paramour of his widowed wife. And not having a concrete plan for the next phase of his life continued to bite him in the ass in unforeseen and unimaginable ways, whether they be at the restaurant, in Babe's steely grasp, or here now in the presence of the street clothes version of one Umberto Craxi, Cardinal of Cosenza.

Frank was disorganized in his thought process at the present moment and therefore at an immediate disadvantage to a man of such a powerful intellect and command of five languages as Cardinal Craxi.

"This was an inspired choice for a location," Craxi said. "Bravo, Mr. Bruno."

"I've always had a fondness for Piazza Sallustio."

"Yes, so must I confess, as well. These are the garden remains of Sallust, a Roman historian who acquired the property after Caesar's death. Eventually a great Cardinal—Ludovico Ludovisi—became the landlord of this area and constructed his villa here."

"I enjoy the bar tucked inside the grounds."

"Ah, you are finder of places and of secrets it seems. Did you receive my letter?"

"Your letter?"

"Yes, I sent it to an address in Niagara Falls, New York. I thought for sure I would hear back from you. But, thankfully, the Ambassador has reached out and found you."

"The letter of excommunication?"

"No, I apologize for the confusion."

"I never read it. My mother received it. She cried the better part of three days."

"Mr. Bruno, in this age of digital communication I have found that letter writing is really the only secure method of correspondence. If you would have read the letter—with your background—you would have understood that I was requesting a meeting and it was not was it purported to be."

"It slipped through the cracks."

"Very well. We are here. Let's get started. Our first, last, and only meeting was under bizarre circumstances. We were all taken aback by that event."

"I'm still sorting it out myself."

"You must have been very good at what you did at the CIA because no one really ever understood the connection between the futures markets and the trading practices of the Church. And *since* that meeting with you, no one has ever learned of these practices. But I still must ask you, why did the United States seem so interested in the Church's trading practices, and why would they have sought us to unwind our positions?"

At that moment, Frank became genuinely alarmed. He fully expected a member of the Italian Secret Service to come straight through a door and put a bullet in his head.

"Yes, this was very surprising to me, Mr. Bruno," Craxi continued. "Not one single news item that would implicate or obfuscate the facts of the situation and make my life entirely unbearable. It is why I am meeting with you now; because nothing has happened since our first meeting."

"Well, I was merely there to give you a warning. I believe that our country has a vested interest in not seeing the Church embroiled in yet another scandal. If it were to come out that you were complicit in the manipulation of the wheat futures market it would not be good at all. There is the age-old dilemma of what role religion should play in society. As far as I know, the United States of America remains a Christian nation, although the recent track record of the Church has made that designation somewhat questionable. Besides, I was there to resign my position."

"So that's why you felt compelled to orchestrate that meeting? A sense of final duty?"

"I am a Catholic, Cardinal. I don't really believe in the Church, however."

"Ah, yes you are. Your mother is a member of St. Mary's in Niagara Falls. That's how I knew where to send you that letter. You attended Catholic grammar and high school."

"Noted."

"Yes, you have a very Catholic pedigree. And you said something in that meeting that has stuck with me all this time and I was hoping you could help clarify this for me."

"Do I walk out that door if I do?"

"Mr. Bruno, you are free to go at any time you like. There is nothing for you to fear."

"OK."

"You mentioned something about that the Church considering a gradual unwinding of its positions in all global commodities markets."

"Yes, I said that."

"But you didn't say how the Church should unwind its positions."

Frank smiled. Maybe he wasn't going to be sacrificed after all.

"Cardinal Craxi, that is beyond my pay grade. I know that it is done all the time but technically, do I know how to do it? No. Absolutely not. I have no organizational affiliation whatsoever. I resigned from the one organization I belonged to. Now, I am a lowly kitchen employee."

"Do you know how much uncertainty I deal with, Mr. Bruno?"

"I would imagine the Church deals with the greatest uncertainty of all."

"And what would that be?"

"The existence of God."

"No, I am afraid that question has been resolved. The greatest uncertainty for any cardinal is who will be the *next* Pope."

"Fascinating."

"Your theories about how and why the Church became involved in the wheat futures market were colorful and elaborate but they were not entirely accurate."

"How so?"

"Well, to begin with, your premise that the Catholic flock is the world's largest consumer of wheat is simply not true. That would be the Arab population."

"I see."

"Yes, this is not widely understood. Or it is understood all too well, depending on your world view. And it would be rather embarrassing if the Church were to be implicated in the next Arab food crisis."

"So, how did you do it?"

"Do what, Mr. Bruno?"

"Unwind those positions."

"Ah, yes. Those were scheduled to be unwound before our meeting. Your warning merely hastened the occurrence and caused me considerable unneeded stress. Our friends at Goldman Sachs were able to offload the positions via derivatives with China, Japan, Korea, and Singapore sovereign wealth funds taking the exposure through structured notes."

"Now you are talking beyond me. I thought you had contempt for Anglo-Saxon finance?"

"Quite the contrary. Had I been born, not in a Catholic country, but somewhere else, I probably would have pursued a career in finance. Do you know what the term "cardinal" stands for in the Church?"

"Prince. You are the princes of the Church."

"Yes. Our main duty is to elect the next Pope. I am not a Cardinal *in pectore,* a secret cardinal appointed by the Pope whose identity is known only to him. I live my life in the Church out in the open. And I do what I do extremely well."

"That being?"

"My job is to understand the world of finance and investments as the Director of the Institute for Religious Works. You call it an investment bank. The Church must survive and to do so it must be engaged in this world of Anglo-Saxon finance. Now, here is where it gets a little challenging. I work for a German. You know Pope Benedict XVI is German and as such he is deeply skeptical of Anglo-Saxon finance.

The Church has always has been involved in real estate and finance in some way or another. But the level of sophistication continues to increase. Still, it is not unlike what Niccolò di Bernardo dei Machiavelli wrote about to another prince, someone not of the Church but who would benefit by an understanding of the role of religion in society, as you seem to have the same appreciation, Mr. Bruno. There are always geopolitical considerations to our decisions regarding where and when to invest. That's why I wanted to meet with you."

"You want me to be your Machiavelli? That is very flattering."

"Well, let's take a look at some things. There are two competing world views at the present moment. There is the current ideation of a free civilized society embodied by the free market process, individual rights, contained within the discipline of the Western democracies whose institutions are supposedly transparent."

"I follow you."

"Yes, then there is the emerging world view of authoritarian capitalism, such as the likes of China."

"What about radical Islam?"

"Not of consequence. It will continue to wreak destruction and havoc but it is not, by any stretch of the imagination, a tenable world view. It is extinct even though it continues to generate its particular breed of mayhem."

"You are starting to confuse me."

"I require someone who can advise me on the political considerations of some of the positions we—the Church—may or may not participate in. Particularly in the matter of food and commodities. The Church has a stated mission to end world hunger. The instability created through the securitization of food commodities creates instability. But it also creates opportunity—if you are on the right side of the trade. Finance is an appropriate response by Western democracies to the threat of Authoritarian Capitalism. It is the only response. Military options are obsolete as the cost of these options will eventually bankrupt our western nations."

"I am a prep cook, not an investment strategist or a geopolitical engineer."

"You have discretion, Mr. Bruno. A prince such as myself seeks discretion in how I operate. In our recent dealings, for example, with China, let's evaluate what has played out. What do you know of China?"

"Well, the two major concerns with China presently are the value of its currency relative to Western currencies and the desire to have them abandon their goal of a blue water navy."

"Ah, those are the strategic goals of the United States and the western democracies of NATO. Those are not the strategic goals of the Church, per se. No, an interesting thing has started to occur in China regarding the underground Roman Church. The state is asserting total control over the Catholic Church there because it is growing faster than in any other country in the world. The state-controlled Catholic Church has appointed bishops without the Pope's approval and forced recognition of these state-sponsored bishops into what is called the Patriotic Chinese Church. Imagine that. The Chinese premier is now in the business of appointing Catholic bishops. Who could have ever imagined? Our challenges will be formidable in China. The starting point might be in Africa. We all know the Chinese are investing heavily in Africa for energy and raw materials. But what about food?"

"I believe the Chinese have an aggressive agriculture program in some of the countries in which they are heavily invested, particularly Angola."

"Well done. You know your field. You see, you are already a Machiavelli. As I told you before, the greatest uncertainty I face—other than the trading positions I am ultimately responsible for on behalf of the Church—is who will be the next Pope. My best guess is that the next Pope will be from Africa, most likely Cardinal Njue, to blunt the Chinese."

"So you're telling me the Church plans to help feed the poor in Africa by investing in the very system that creates massive instability in the food markets?"

"That's one way of looking at it. The longer view of commodities is that they are all running out as population grows. The indexing of commodities is a fact of life and one we ignore at our peril. Authoritarian capitalism leaves no room for the Roman church. Our fate is inextricably bound to the world view that allows for freedom of choice to participate in the religion of one's choosing. A prince or a president or a premiere cannot be overly religious but he rules better when his citizenry is; whether in a western democracy or in an authoritarian regime."

"That *is* Machiavellian."

"I would suggest some reading for you if you decide to work with me."

"The Prince?"

"No. You have probably already read that in your school years. I would recommend a lesser known work by Machiavelli, the *Life of Castruccio Castracani*. It's the story of a prince who was abandoned as a baby in a cornfield but who, through guile and talent, achieved near-greatness in his lifetime. Near-greatness."

"I believe I am familiar with such a story."

The meeting concluded with an agreement to continue discussions the following day to determine what, if any, level of commitment Frank Bruno could give to Cardinal Umberto Craxi in this newly created position. This left Frank the rest of the evening to fade into the backdrop of Piazza Sallustio; to take in a meal at his favorite Roman restaurant Cantina Cantarini, completely content without having to venture out into the greater city itself and deal with the barbarian Romans.

He turned left into the Piazza hungry for a plate of sautéed chicory from his favorite local restaurant. He would order fish—and lots of it—and drink some wine while contemplating the events of the day. Could this be the opportunity to set up shop in this beloved space; to cash in on the past twenty years of government service? Whatever commissions he earned in the employ of Cardinal Craxi would be a pittance next to those generated by Goldman Sachs, et al. He was in position to do well, perhaps, at least less harm and it intrigued him.

When he arrived at the entrance to the restaurant, Frank was crestfallen. It was closed; not as in for the evening but out of business entirely. Cantina Cantarini had operated at this location for over thirty years and was consistently mobbed by tourists and locals alike. It was always listed in guides as the epitome of a Roman *trattoria.* Its modest sign was an essential signpost of the Piazza. It was impossible for Frank to conceive that it was gone.

On the front door there was an official notice of repossession. From where—the City of Rome? From whom? Was it a landlord dispute? Tax issues? Had the family simply thrown in the towel, exhausted from the years of operation?

Frank felt panicked. A restaurant going dark is a

common occurrence but, to those who have worked in the business, there is always a minor tragedy lurking in the taking place of such an occurrence.

The world was a cold, inhospitable place, Frank thought. If he were to do anything with Cardinal Craxi he would demand six months of compensation up-front.

Suddenly, his cell phone vibrated, alerting him to a text message from, of all people, Cousin Leonard Krolewski.

"Babe has been a rested...Should I open the restaurant."

FIFTEEN

Frank arrived back to a media circus of proportions that dwarfed the original coverage of the death of Chef Joe Bass. The story had crossed over into a salacious soup of cable television headlines and was now served across a broad spectrum of channels that had heretofore carried only sporadic coverage of the initial incident.

Babe's mugshot, juxtaposed to a cross-dissolve of glam shots of her in the restaurant, received full treatment on Nancy Grace the evening of her arrest, bumping the disappearance of a Texas cheerleader to bottom of the hour of the TV tabloid show.

There were no jawbones to uncover or DNA results pending in the arrest of Barbara La Bruna for the charge of voluntary manslaughter in the first degree. The only things lacking, which would have made make the event truly viral, was a collective failure by the media to peg Babe with a moniker equal to the degree of the crime she had been indicted on, and the striking visual image she portrayed in her black outfit, shackled in handcuffs being led out of the restaurant, in front of high definition video cameras.

The banal "Black Widow Killer" would have to suffice for now, assigned according to the decree of cable television's foremost raconteur of America's murderous phenotypic character, Nancy Grace.

Niagara County District Attorney William A. Cooperman stepped to the microphone for the assemble local press conference in Babe's arraignment.

"We are here to announce that Barbara Athena La Bruna has been charged with voluntary manslaughter in the first degree killing of Giuseppe Basi, both of the City of Niagara Falls, New York. Mrs. La Bruna was arrested at her business this evening by Detectives Nathan Sensabaugh and Joseph Steck. Mrs. La Bruna has been remanded to the Niagara County Jail in contemplation of a bail hearing scheduled for tomorrow in front of Judge Constance Wolfgang. The arrest of Mrs. La Bruna marks the completion of diligent and difficult police work by Detectives Sensabaugh and Steck and other members of the Niagara Falls Police force, and members of these offices as well. We will now take a limited number of questions."

"What was the break in the case that led to this sudden turn of events?"

"There was a recent development in the investigation of the restaurant's finances by state tax examiners that helped lead us to a conclusion that Mrs. La Bruna was involved in her husband's death. That's all I can say on that subject for now."

"But Mrs. La Bruna was reported to be outside of the restaurant at the time of her husband's murder?"

"I'll take this one," Police Chief Armando Esposito stepped forward. "That is actually incorrect. Mrs. La Bruna was indeed identified as being at the Haeberle Plaza branch of HSBC Bank the morning of the homicide but according to the coroner's report we believe there was an ample window of opportunity in which she could have committed the crime."

"But what about the cell phone call she received from the employee at the restaurant who discovered the body?"

"The bank is a mere two blocks away from the restaurant; less than a five minute drive by car. Mrs. La Bruna was wearing a long winter overcoat that morning," District Attorney Cooperman said. When officers arrived at the scene they observed Mrs. La Bruna kneeling over the body. Her clothing had a large amount of the victim's blood on it. The employee, Mr. Krolewski, has stated that the couple was engaged in an argument that morning. We believe that during the course of the trial we will reveal the nature of that argument and provide the jury with evidence of Mrs. La Bruna's motive in the slaying of her husband."

"Has Mrs. La Bruna confessed to the killing?"

"No, she has not."

"Has she retained counsel?"

"Yes she has. I believe she has—Attorney George Augstell from Buffalo—but you will have to check those facts for yourself."

"Has anyone visited with her?"

"No one as of yet. She is still being processed in the county jail."

"What about the theory of robbery?"

"Nothing in our investigation has pointed to anything other than the victim of this crime, Mr. Basi, knowing his assailant."

"Does this mean Mrs. La Bruna has always been a suspect, contrary to past police statements?"

"Yes, she has; from day one."

Frank made it to the county jailhouse just in time to hear Big George Augstell's first public statements to the crush of cameras and microphones dwarfed by his six foot-eight frame. There was only one Big George Augstell in Niagara County. He was the towering attorney who represented the most high profile cases of murder and recidivism in a town full such of occurrences; his hands a pair of catcher's mitts, his stride double that of ordinary men.

Big George generally liked to be paid partly in cash. Frank's secondary objective in visiting the jailhouse was to do just that—hand Big George Augstell a big, brown paper bag of cash in the backseat of his Lincoln Navigator.

First, however, Frank stepped to the side of the assembled press corps and listened.

"My client, Barbara La Bruna, emphatically denies any involvement in the death of her husband, Giuseppe Basi. The past eight months have been an extremely difficult time for my client and now the bizarre judgment of our local police department and the District Attorney's Office has combined to create a complete miscarriage of justice—a justice that we look forward to correcting sooner, rather than later. We are confident these charges will be dropped and this case will never see the inside of the courtroom."

"Mr. Augstell, can you tell us about the investigation into the restaurant's finances that, according to police, led them to identify your client's motive for the murder?"

"I believe the charge is manslaughter in the first degree; let's keep the facts straight. As to your question, it is my understanding that the State Department of Taxation and Finance is auditing all restaurants in the area; not just my client's. Every single restaurant and cash business in this city, county, and state are under the microscope of an agency that is anxious to wring every dollar out of small business. So you tell me, how this could lead our District Attorney to the wild assumption of Mrs. La Bruna's culpability in the manslaughter of her husband?"

"Police Chief Esposito said that your client had enough time to commit the manslaughter and cover it up. How do you respond?"

"Mrs. La Bruna was the person who telephoned police that morning. She was in the ambulance with her husband when he passed away. To posit the theory that she planned his death in advance—and to a man nearly one hundred pounds heavier than she—is quite far-fetched, wouldn't you say?"

"Does your client have a statement for us?"

"Yes; I am glad you asked that," Big George said, reaching for a slip of paper in his coat pocket. Big George was not entirely freelancing here, even though the paper contained the odd scribbling of his OCD brain and not the verbatim words Babe had ended their first client/attorney jailhouse conference with.

But they were close enough.

"Yes; my client wants everyone to know that Restaurant Giuseppe Basi will be open for business soon, and she expects to be there to greet all of her customers at the hostess station. All reservations will be honored. An automatic gratuity of twenty percent will be added to tables of eight or more. There will be two specials: a Maine lobster risotto and venison medallions. The early bird special comes with a choice of soup or salad but not both. There is parking in the rear of the restaurant for your convenience. No coffee or dessert is served tableside. A separate area in the bar has been reserved for this as she believes, along with her late husband Joe, that coffee should be consumed in the standing position. And she is innocent of this charge. Thank you."

"Has your client mentioned her husband's gambling debts?"

"And you are?"

"Hayden Buckingham, *The Buck Stopped Here.*"

"We have discussed many aspects of their relationship but I will not speak publicly about any of those conversations."

"What about Chef Joe Bass's publicly-embarrassing appearance on national television and his tabloid lifestyle? Has Mrs. La Bruna mentioned any of that?"

"No, Ms. Buckingham; she has not. Perhaps you could shed some light on this at another time."

It was unlike Big George to make a tactical error in a press conference, yielding a clear audio channel to some voice other than his own booming baritone; yet perhaps even he had never been in this much key light, or in front of so many lines of vertical resolution.

"Or anything about his numerous girlfriends, his cocaine problem, his fast and loose spending of money?"

"You forgot to mention his bitchin' Camaro," a local reporter from the *Niagara Gazette* and personal acquaintance of Chef chimed in.

"And that maybe Babe La Bruna had just had enough. You can only be embarrassed and humiliated for so long before you finally snap and try to protect what you have built up over the years. Everyone assumes it's your husband who is responsible for your success but that's really not the case at all. Somehow, in some way, you've managed to be successful in spite of your famous husband who really does not understand the first thing about business. He's really just a child seeking fame and approval from whatever venue offers it—television, food, slutty women, fast cars, drugs, gambling."

"I didn't know you worked for the District Attorney, Ms. Buckingham. Is that your opening statement?"

"It's just a working theory. But I can see something like that coming to the surface," Hayden did not break her gaze at Big George, who looked confused and slightly wounded by the ambush.

"Well, if that's your case, I look forward to ripping it to shreds in a court of law," Big George said, regaining his composure and pushing his way to the Navigator.

"I thought you said you expected an early dismissal?" Hayden said, following him to the driver's side of the vehicle. It was only the smoked glass of the car's windows that prevented her from identifying Frank in the back seat.

"What a crafty little bitch, that Buckingham," Big George said. "How you doing Frank? It's been a long time, hasn't it?"

"Has to be. I lost track of you before law school."

"Yes; I thought you were in the CIA or something like that?"

"Did my mother tell you that?"

"Come to think of it, she did. She sees my mother at church every now and again."

"My mother, I believe, loves to publicize my career path."

"Don't they all? I still live with mine. Well, sort of."

That was the other thing about Big George. He was often referred to as Big Gay George Augstell, the town's most openly homosexual six foot-eight attorney. But no one ever called him that to his face.

Frank vividly remembered the time Big George busted up a bar patron for committing just such an indiscretion. Big George asked this fellow to step outside, rolled up the sleeves of his immaculately pressed Ralph Lauren polo dress shirt and, before he wiped the street clean with this unwitting gay-basher, he'd had the courtesy to inform him that the only thing he liked more than sucking cock was kicking ass.

"What about this Buckingham? How much does she know about Babe and Frank?"

"I would assume most everything."

"They that close?"

"They were close. Probably not anymore. I think Babe is gonna flip when she sees Buckingham's next show."

"She really can't miss it. She's been on ever since the arrest. It's like she's trying to out-duel Nancy Grace."

"I'd bet on Buckingham. She knows just about everything that went on in that restaurant and between Babe and Joe."

"So what she said back there; is it plausible?"

"Yes, it's plausible. But I never once believed Babe killed Joe. If she did, then I am a complete fool."

"What about this tax audit? Did Babe ever clue you in on the restaurant financials? Could she really be sitting on that big a pile?"

"I don't know."

"Well, I need to know. I need to know how much, where it's hidden, and, if she did it to Joe, how it happened; and I really need to know that soon."

"What did she tell you?"

"She said she was innocent. That someone should call you for my retainer and that was about it. Then she launched into some crazy rant about the restaurant still being open. It's like that was the first and only thing on her mind."

"When will she be out?"

"I expect tomorrow. The hearing has been moved to the afternoon. Bail should not be a problem. She's clean."

"I have your retainer."

Big George applied the brakes to the Navigator. The sting of childhood poverty had never really healed inside him. He had no reason to make the arrangements in such a manner but the ritual that preceded his handling of a major case was always the same.

He could not work unless he physically counted the proceeds of his retainer. This meant that his secretary, Delores, had to first cash clients' checks, deliver the money in an envelope to Big George in his office for a physical count, and then redeposit the total amount back into his bank account. It was not about any sort of tax evasion, duplicity, or dirty dealing; it was merely that Big George needed to touch and feel something real before he started work. Once he counted twice, and the numbers matched up, that's all he would need to fight to the death to secure the release of his clients.

SIXTEEN

In Frank's limited dealings with the incarcerated, he was always struck by how penal architecture and clothing had a shrinking effect on its inhabitants. Perhaps it was their gradual dehydration that caused this, he theorized, but such was not the case with Babe La Bruna when he visited her in the morning prior to her first court appearance.

She appeared defiant.

There were only a few hours before the hearing in Judge Connie Wolfgang's courtroom and yet all Babe wanted to talk about was the bucket list of items required to reopen Restaurant Giuseppe Basi.

"Did you order fresh flowers for the tables?"

"Babe, that can wait."

"I'll be out of here by three o'clock. We're opening for dinner tonight."

"No we are not. It will be a disaster. Nothing is

prepped and when I say that, I mean you. You are not prepared. The server schedule has not been posted. Nobody has answered the phone in three days. We are not opening."

"Then I'll do it without you. Kenny did a good job on sauté while you were gone. The crew can handle it. As a matter of fact, you've done your job so well in training a new kitchen staff there's no need for you to stay on any longer. And there's Leonard; he knows every recipe."

"Fabulous. But let's just get through this court appearance right now."

"Frank, there's no way they're gonna make this charge stick. Do you know what Sensabaugh told me? He said a lot of people did not like the way I acted after Joe's death. He said I was flouting tragedy. That's why they hauled me in. He said I should have just closed up the restaurant, kept a low profile, and gone about my business. But the restaurant is my business."

"What about this financial stuff? What's that all about?"

"So it appears the State tax department has had counters at the restaurant for the past month. They have a daily, weekly, and monthly tally of customers in the dining room, at the bar, of liquor inventory purchases and our food purchases. They're saying my numbers don't match up based on the volume the restaurant does. They think I'm hiding money."

"Well, Babe, you are."

"Shut the fuck up, Frank," Babe snarled.

No restaurateur wants to be told the obvious—that they are hiding money. Modern governments beholden to massive deficit-financing breed the most virulent strain of justification of partial compliance among their small business constituency. Small businesses understand that there is no bailout for them if they fail; they are not too big to fail—just big enough to be plundered by the insatiable appetite of government.

"It's time for you to go. Goodbye. I did not kill my husband. That's what you need to know. They are just trying to squeeze me any way they can. But it won't work. Did you take care of Big George?"

"All set. Calm down. You're going to appear before Judge Wolfgang. You have to focus on that and that only. Big George said there will be cameras in the court room and you have to be the epitome of—"

"They did it in front of the customers," Babe interrupted. "They did it right at seven o'clock when the dining room was full. They came right through the front door and cuffed me in front of the staff and the customers."

"Was Lo Piccolo behind the tax audit?"

"Yes. He sang like a canary on all of us. It's just not me. It's just about everybody in the business. This has been going on for weeks. I didn't want to tell you."

"You're going to need a good tax lawyer. Big George is strictly criminal defense. I'll ask him for a recommendation."

"We have to move some things."

"I know."

"No you don't. They plan on searching the premises, again. The entire premises, including the basement. Lo Piccolo knows about the room, or at least he's heard of it. His dad used to run around there with all the goombahs back in the day."

"Let's get you out of here first."

Bail was set at $100,000 for the release of Babe La Bruna despite the protestations of Big George Augstell for a lesser amount. The La Bruna defense team was doubly blindsided when Judge Wolfgang signed an order requiring Babe to surrender her U.S. passport along with the bail bond. True enough, the restaurant stood just blocks away from the Canadian border. Judge Wolfgang claimed she wanted to remove any temptation for weekend trips (or longer, her exact words) to Nova Scotia—or anywhere else above the 49th parallel—by Babe in her company-leased Mercedes Benz.

Judge Wolfgang was the host of a local cable access show called *The Law and You,* and not only were television cameras going to be allowed into her courtroom to record every petition and proceeding in the matter of the People v. La Bruna, but the judge's staff was actively seeking larger quarters with increased electrical amperage to accommodate all of the video crews.

This was Judge Connie Wolfgang's moment to bask in the limelight of cable networks after having to sit her bony ass on a pine chair during the past thirty years in judgment of parochial welfare fraud cases, DWIs, petit larcenies, breaking and enterings, and simple and aggravated assaults. She was not about to repeat the mistakes of that douche bag, Lance Ito. There would be clarity from the start in her courtroom. She had already speed-dialed one of her best friends, a drug rep from Allergan, who was coming over to her house that evening for a Botox party.

As surprising and eventful as the bail hearing played out, the image of Babe La Bruna standing before Judge Constance Wolfgang served as mere B-roll to the dramatic wide-shot of her outside the courtroom, lunging in the direction of Hayden Buckingham.

Catfight.

If you had scrolled back the footage, you would have seen that Hayden Buckingham stood her ground at the start of the fisticuffs, giving as good as she was getting, but in the end Babe La Bruna overwhelmed her with a flurry of rights and lefts that slumped the honeysuckle starlet of food and celebrity.

Nobody, including the courthouse deputies, were anxious to jump in. Everybody loves a good catfight, right? It's up there with two highly-skilled professional hockey players tossing off their gloves and going at it. Surprisingly little hair was pulled out in the melee between Babe and Hayden but bite marks were exchanged. Their fists were closed from the onset of the violence. These were real punches; overhand rights, uppercuts, jabs and a left hook that came out of nowhere—as all devastating left hooks do—which delivered the decisive TKO.

Hayden Buckingham addressed the top of the hour satellite feed for the Food Network, Discovery Channel and CNN's *Headline News* straight from the back of an ambulance with a bed sheet draped to disguise—and with the proper back lighting to suggest—the process of her getting a tetanus shot right in her superb ass.

"And so concludes a dramatic first day in the arraignment and bail hearing of Babe La Bruna, charged for the manslaughter of her husband, celebrity chef Joe Bass. As a reporter, it's not often I have found myself inserted directly into the middle of a fast emerging story. But you can be sure that I will be here until there is a verdict in the case; until justice is served, whatever that may be. This is Hayden Buckingham, outside of the City courtroom in Niagara Falls, New York. The Buck Stopped Here."

SEVENTEEN

A restaurant is similar to an airplane in that it does not benefit from disuse. It must be open when other businesses are not, during storms, holidays, weekends, national wars, local causes of celebration. It is indifferent to all of these external considerations and adheres only to an internal imperative to be open and generating income. When it is not open or in operation, things fall apart, like an airplane left too long on the tarmac.

But an airplane is not fragile. It cannot be fragile, whereas a restaurant, such as Restaurant Giuseppe Basi, is the very definition of fragility.

There is a whole class of restaurants that has arisen out of man's attempt to engineer the fragility out of them. They are called chain restaurants. You know them. You have eaten from them, despite your better judgment, because there have been times when you are simply too bereft of imagination to consider any alternatives.

The model for building a chain restaurant relies on an assembly of "best practices" from the foodservice industry, strung together in a codified manual of operations, financed, then unwound in the form of paramilitary operations and measured by metrics that are comprehensible even to a simpleton.

They are also a collection of our worst fears and worst assumptions of our evolution.

It does not make sense that we should actively seek out our nutrition delivered in this manner but somehow chain restaurants evolved right alongside man, feeding our desire to no longer feed ourselves. But we know that evolution is capable of trickery and treachery, just like the restaurant business, which can fool us into a reliance on something that will ultimately lead to our undoing.

At least that is how Frank thought of fragility. A great restaurant cannot exist but for an infinitesimal moment in time. Degradation, variance, sloppiness, and exhaustion are all bound to creep in at some moment, robbing the truly great restaurant of its greatness. Outwardly, this decline may not be apparent to customers for months, even years. Restaurateurs can guard themselves against it, and in the process develop a particular type of neurosis that compels them to open more restaurants; deceiving themselves into believing that a new concept or a new menu will alleviate the grinding routine of serving food for profit.

Then there is the vast middle of mediocre restaurants. Restaurants in that vast middle are often rewarded, and rather handsomely so. Rarely are the extremes of exceptionality rewarded in the restaurant industry—truly great restaurants can never earn an appropriate margin equal to the pain and suffering put forth to achieve such greatness. This remains so due to the inescapable role of randomness. One can never be certain—or, better stated, less certain—of how many people will walk through one's doors on any given night.

These were among Frank's thoughts as he keyed his way into the dark restaurant the morning after Babe was released on bail and forced to surrender her passport. He did not smell leaking gas the way Chef did on the morning of his death. But he did smell something equally offensive to the sensibility of someone in the restaurant business; he smelled the rot and stench of an unemptied deep fat fryer.

Cousin Leonard had fucked up.

Rule 101 of restaurant closing held that to maintain the integrity of one's fryer oil it had to be emptied and strained nightly, the vats scrubbed with a mixture of common white vinegar and water, and the oil covered for later re-use. The phenomenal popularity of the restaurant's fried calamari, the frittura di pesci, and the taglio delle verdure depended on this essential procedure. Frank guessed that the spent grease must have been sitting in the fryer for the past five days of closure, decaying ever so rapidly.

As Frank walked through the dining room, the secret filth of the restaurant increased exponentially inside of him. Restaurants are a filthy business, even the clean ones. This was not his restaurant and yet the failure of the kitchen crew to execute one simple task at closing had prompted Frank Bruno to consider turning around, locking the door, and catching the next plane to Rome, ready to start whatever assignment the nefarious Cardinal Craxi had in store for him.

Instead, he moved onward to the kitchen.

Cousin Leonard arrived an hour later, his key chain dangling from his hip, the smell of five days of inconsequential drinking upon his breath. Give Cousin Leonard his due. He never once surrendered a shift in the restaurant due to an over consumption of alcohol.

"You didn't strain the fryers and you left the grease uncovered. We're gonna have to scrub them down and change the oil out. It's toast."

"Forgot."

"I want you to take a look in the walk-in and put together a prep list. We're probably going to have to pitch some things. They've been sitting for five days."

"Frank, you know I can't write. Joe always made the prep list"

"Then how did you read it?"

"He'd tell me what to do and I'd remember. Sometimes, I'd forget."

"Christ, Leonard. Make some coffee."

Frank immediately felt shame for his lack of tact and compassion with Cousin Leonard. But he recognized his sentiments of the moment might also be one of those evolutionary deceptions.

How many of the illiterate had died poor and destitute?

Probably the majority. Rationality argued that to be literate increased one's chances of survival but by the looks of Cousin Leonard, Frank reasoned, he would outlive them all.

"All right, we've got a lot of work to do," Frank said. "Basically, it's a restock situation. I need you to go downstairs and start with the pasta. Then we need steaks cut, burgers ground, osso buco set up. I need the lamb racks trimmed. I need all the breads made. I've got some nice Pompano coming in today. I need you to filet it."

"I'm on it, Boss."

Frank grabbed a kitchen apron, his knife kit, turned on the radio, and got to work. He opened the kitchen door to allow a fresh breeze to pass through the screen door. Deliveries would be arriving soon and this would hasten the process, eliminating the need to constantly stop what he was doing to receive the goods.

Prepping food in the early morning hours of a closed restaurant was a unique moment of luxury and solitude. There was nothing left to learn about the base recipes of Restaurant Giuseppe Basi. There was only the repetition of them and this was what professional cooking was all about, repetition.

For instance, he could render the mirepoix for the ragù al' coniglio for the hundredth time, and it would never cease to amaze him that when it was done right how translucent the carrot, celery, and fennel became, surrendering into the pan, before the white wine was added.

Frank had never felt the presence of the deceased before. It was only in the bits and scraps of our brains, he surmised, that we kept the dead alive; soon to be deglazed away from wherever in our cranial meat locker they were held in cold storage, thawed by the scent of fresh rosemary or basil, or released in a fully coherent memory by the perfume of a sauce simmering upon the stove.

He succumbed for a moment to the total and complete recall of Joe Bass.

That's when Frank knew he had but a week to complete his duties at the restaurant. He was leaving. It lightened and lifted his spirit. He had often witnessed chefs on the very last stages of their kitchen assignments, suddenly buoyed by the prospects of imminent departure.

It was as if they were reborn when the burden of their station was about to be released. Their bad habits disappeared. No more shortcuts or short tempers or shouting. There were smiles everywhere. Everyone forced to work alongside them had to endure the fact that they were leaving while the rest of the crew had to stay, work, and repeat the same thing, over and over.

Frank looked up from his prep table and smiled. In the back door walked his fish delivery. He quickly checked in the order of shrimp, squid, scallops, mussels, clams, and the thirty pounds of fresh pompano.

"I see that Rothman is still trying to charge for ice," Frank said as he weighed the pompano out of the box. "This is twenty seven five. Take a look."

The deliveryman bent over and looked at the scale.

"You zero that thing out?"

"Go fuck yourself. And tell Rothman to send his kids through college some other way than charging us for ice."

The deliveryman laughed.

"I'll adjust the bill. But I got to call it in and get the approval."

Frank called downstairs while his invoice was adjusted to reflect the true weight of his pompano delivery.

"Leonard, get up here."

"What's up, Boss?"

"Fish is in. Clean it. Ice it down. Then I need you to clean the pompano."

"The boss says hello and asks that you call him sometime for a card game," the deliveryman told Frank.

Cousin Leonard grabbed the cases of newly delivered fish. He had to make two trips downstairs before he could start breaking them down. Joe Bass was fanatic on the storage of seafood; the arrival of a new delivery of such product at Restaurant Giuseppe Basi carried the same gravity as that of a freshly harvested organ for transplant.

Get it on ice, now!

Chef kept his shellfish tags in a monthly folder and made Babe enter them in a spreadsheet at the end of a week. His calamari was fresh, so it needed to be cleaned, cut, and portioned into bags but only in the amount that would be used that evening. If the restaurant ran out of portions during service, more would be cut to order.

All shellfish was thoroughly washed in the designated fish sink downstairs. Then it was stored in drainable plastic containers so that the ice placed over the top of the shellfish would not pool, but instead funnel its way into an elaborate PVC drain system Chef had personally rigged in his cooler.

Once that was done, Cousin Leonard took his razor-sharp boning knife out and began to filet the pompano. The specials list for the evening would trumpet the sustainable character of the pompano but the reality of the situation was that it was three dollars per pound cheaper than the non-sustainable Chilean sea bass and it would sell for about the same price.

Cousin Leonard's knife skills were unrivaled in the restaurant. They were his greatest source of pride, superior even to those of Chef Joe Bass, who was no slouch practitioner of kitchen cutlery gymnastics.

It was in the cleaning and gutting of fish where Cousin Leonard truly shined. He had an incredible ability to yield the most consistent portions from the fleshy bellies of fish, enabling the restaurant to receive a maximum return on investment and buy whole, rather than by the piece or by the side. Often when Cousin Leonard would render a bucket of bones from meat or seafood that he had just butchered, Frank would stare in amazement at the technical precision of Cousin Leonard's knife work.

The dismantling of the pompano that would have taken even the most experienced fishmonger a considerable amount of time to process took Cousin Leonard only thirty minutes. He blew through it and layered the filets side-by-side with deli wax paper, lining up each portion of the fish in plastic tubs for Frank to inspect. He kept the entrails, bones, heads, tails, and fins in a five gallon bucket for fish fume that would be made later on.

Cousin Leonard's hangover had started to throb. He bounded up the steps with the fish in one hand, carried like a tray of cocktails, and his boning knife in the other, putting too much thought and effort into where he was going, but not enough in the manner in which he was carrying that knife.

He was certain of only one thing; that he needed another cup of coffee and to shove a couple of ibuprofens down his pie hole from the first-aid kit next to the kitchen walk-in cooler.

Frank, at the same time, was in the kitchen walk-in cooler. He was inventorying his prepped and pared items with a clipboard and pencil. He could not determine if a particular tub of chicken breast had gone off so he put down the clipboard and grabbed it.

He smelled them.

Not good.

But he thought he should clean them before he made any decisions regarding whether they should be thrown out.

Professional kitchens are a truly dangerous place. Injuries occur all the time. Cuts, grease splatters, slips, falls, back strains, scalding, dismemberment, even death.

So there Frank could be seen on the newly installed kitchen security camera, walking out of the walk-in cooler, while at that precise moment in time Cousin Leonard approached the side panels of the walk-in cooler from the opposite direction at a reckless pace.

The kitchen blind spot.

Cousin Leonard's boning knife grazed Frank' right side then traveled downward in the collision of their bodies, plunging into his thigh. The tubs of chicken and fish went flying everywhere. So did Cousin Leonard and Frank, as the boning knife became a part of Frank Bruno's flesh instead of Cousin Leonard's hand.

"Shit, I'm bleeding," Frank said, as he stood up.

He knew immediately that he would require stitches. He looked at Cousin Leonard, still fumbling on the floor searching for his glasses. He grabbed him by the shoulders and shook him.

"Leonard, did you stab Joe? It was you who killed him, wasn't it?"

Cousin Leonard was trembling, and not from the recent collision. His glasses were a complete mess of first-aid tape and fish scale residue. He was a man nearly forty years of age but mentally still a child; a child who had been caught in a lie.

"Yes, I did, Frank."

"Oh, my God. Leonard why haven't you said anything?"

"Nobody asked me. I was too a scared. On 'count of my accident."

"What happened? Leonard. It's OK, please tell me."

"My mother says if I lose my SSI disability and my welfare check on 'count of me working under the table for Joe and Babe, we'd have nothing to survive on. We only survive now on account of me working under the table and collecting my SSI disability and my welfare and food stamps."

"Did you accidentally stab Joe with a kitchen knife, like you almost did to me now?"

"No Frank. I stabbed you, too. You're bleeding."

"I know that, Leonard, but how did it happen with Joe?"

"Well I turned the corner and Joe just barreled into me. I had a knife in my hand and I think I raised my hand up—ya know—like a reflex or something. It happened so fast."

"It went into his chest?"

"It went in all the way," Cousin Leonard said, tears streaming down his face. "I felt it go in."

"Then what did you do?"

"I made it worse. I tried to take it out."

"Jesus Christ, Leonard."

"Joe told me to grab his cell phone in the office cubbyhole and call an ambulance."

"Did you?"

"No. I don't know how to call an ambulance on a cell phone. I kept punching in numbers and finally Babe's came up and before you know it she was answering and I was crying. I told her what happened to Joe. She said she was on her way. But when Joe saw the blood coming out of his mouth, he started to panic and he tried to stand up."

"Does Babe know you did this?"

"Yes."

"Why didn't you tell the police?

"She knows I didn't mean it, Frank. It was an accident. I loved Joe. I loved him. He was my cousin. I worked right beside him since the day the restaurant opened. He paid me on Tuesdays in cash on 'count of my accident… when I was a baby… and they dropped me on my head."

EIGHTEEN

Despite a preponderance of evidence to the contrary, Babe La Bruna indeed stood trial for the manslaughter of her husband, an unconventional legal strategy that she alone decided upon, despite the adamant protestations of a defense team headed by Big George Augstell, who was completely unglued by the fact that she was not guilty and that he had never before represented an innocent defendant in all his years of trial law.

Big George demanded a doubling of his retainer before he would sign off on Babe's controversial course of action.

It's one thing to roll into court and give it your best bloody shot. That's what Big George lived for. But he did so under the total and complete understanding that his clients were guilty as sin itself and it was his job—the job he was born to do—to make these assumptions dissolve in the eyes of the jury. Big George did this spectacularly well because he had the unique ability to make everyone in the courtroom—judge, jury, district attorney, and audience—all guilty of something along with the defendant sitting next to him. This was his trademark defense, and in that moment of collective guilt, Big George kicked down the doors of plausible deniability and put a giant bear hug around the jury.

But Babe La Bruna had turned this logic on its head and confounded Big George by refusing to allow Cousin Leonard to give his statement to the police. It was all an elaborate stalling tactic by Babe to buy more time to defend herself against the massive tax evasion charges that were about to be leveled her way on top of whatever else the state and federal government could throw against the wall and make it stick to her.

"We are all guilty of one thing or another, aren't we Big George? I've heard you say it a million times," Babe told him in the Lincoln Navigator. "I might as well get my one judgment of innocence on the record before they crucify me."

"We're going to let them have at it then," Big George said, finally warming up to the idea after he counted his second cash retainer. "When it's our turn, I'm going to do something I have not done since I was fresh out of law school and didn't know any better."

"What's that?"

"I'm going to put you on the stand, Babe."

"Brilliant."

"Oh, yes. You're going to tell them exactly what happened."

"Do I have to bring Leonard into this? He's already terrified of losing his benefits and being forced to repay all the years he worked for us under the table. Not to mention the taxes I'll be dinged for on it."

"I don't see any other way."

"What if you just ask me if I did it, straight up?"

"Then what?"

"That's it. Try it."

Big George watched Babe deliver her mock testimony in his plush conference room. He watched very carefully—her eyes, her face, the contraction of her jaw, the position of her shoulders—and he determined, in that instant, that one line of testimony was nearly good enough. And if it was not, he would improvise on the spot.

"Barbara La Bruna, did you stab your husband, Giuseppe Basi, on the morning of January eleventh, in your restaurant kitchen and allow him to bleed to his death?"

"No. I most emphatically did not."

It took Frank a lot longer to come around to Babe's way of thinking on all of this. He was certain she had nothing to do with Joe's death. He listened to her describe how she had decided, in the ambulance while Joe was dying, that this was a terrible accident and that she would not reveal Cousin Leonard's part in it unless absolutely necessary.

Live and work long enough in the restaurant business and you are conditioned to expect the very worst. You cannot prepare for it. But it's always there, Babe lamented, and even then there is still a way around a bad situation. This is the ultimate lesson of the restaurant business, she said.

It was her decision alone to allow her husband's death to remain an unanswered act of random evil. That is what the death of Chef Joe Bass remained; a very remote statistical improbability but a possibility nonetheless.

It was also good for business.

It was good for business in a Paul Castellano-meets-the-sidewalk-outside-of-Sparks Steakhouse kinda way. Or, by any other metric in the restaurant business—tables turned, check average, food-to-booze comparison (booze was way up), same-day-sales, same-period-sales, year-to-date, even dessert sales (a category that was previously negative), and then, of course, the key indicator at Restaurant Giuseppe Basi, Canadian dollar counts.

She demanded Frank answer two questions: will you tell the Police what happened? And, will you help me move the cash and gold out of the basement?

"I'll help you with the second part first," Frank said. "I'm still thinking about the first part."

"Good enough. You probably realize I didn't tell the police about Cousin Leonard for selfish reasons as well," Babe said.

"How so?" Frank was stopped dead his tracks by Babe's offhand remark.

"Think about it. Joe was dead. Leonard was the only one who knew how to run the kitchen. He was the only one who knew how to make the food. I couldn't have reopened without him here."

Frank was shocked at his own naiveté.

Of course, she could not have reopened. That's why she wanted Frank there; to extract all of the knowledge Joe had imparted to Cousin Leonard and to write it all down, recipe it, and then train the new staff.

"That's kind of cold."

"I did what I did. What are you going to do?"

This was not Frank's restaurant. He did not see any other solution

"Help you move that money," he said.

"How?"

"First we get it off premises. Then we figure out where to put it."

"Any ideas?"

"There's only one place to put it. Switzerland."

"I don't have a passport, remember?"

"There are ways around that. There are people for that."

"You know any of those people?"

"I know many of those people. But after this is done, I am on my way outta here. And we have to do something for Joe."

"Joe?"

"He's in a crematorium vat above the bar. It's disgraceful."

"Not in some Catholic cemetery, Frank. Don't even mention it. He would haunt us the rest of our lives."

"Then think about somewhere else. Somewhere he

liked to go. Then I'll give you my answer about whether I'll tell the police about Cousin Leonard."

NINETEEN

One of the first people Bruno thought of was Cardinal Craxi. He contacted Ambassador Reed and told him to inform the Cardinal that he was available for freelance assignment. His conditions of employment were relatively modest: he requested an apartment in Piazza Sallustio, paid in advance for the year, and a salary of two hundred thousand dollars, also paid in advance to a Swiss bank account.

His last request remained puzzling to the delighted cardinal but ultimately doable.

A Vatican passport arrived via FedEx in the name of Regina Ornella Carruana, a native of Malta, aged forty-two, with a photograph supplied by Frank of a starkly beautiful woman possessing dark black hair, a scar below her chin, and deep olive brown eyes, who at other times had been known as Barbara Athena La Bruna.

Restaurant Giuseppe Basi remained dark in the

three month period leading up to trial but a For Sale sign was not bolted onto the western facade until Babe actually stepped into the courtroom flanked by Big George.

Her plan of stalling for time was working. She had received a six-month delay in all of the state auditing actions pending an outcome of her criminal trial. Calls from real estate brokers who represented thinly disguised third parties, mostly from the camp of Bebe Lo Piccolo, inquired about the For Sale sign once it went live on the restaurant building.

By the time Babe took the stand in her defense, Frank had already completed his first assignment for Cardinal Craxi in the remotest reaches of Zambia. It was a rather mundane venture to assess the lay of the land in this poorest of poor nations. He did not learn anything that he did not already know about Zambia to report back to the cardinal, except a nugget or two of information that had minimal commercial potential.

Apparently, there was a huge influx of Emery Thompson batch freezers into the sub-Sahara. These are the machines that were first—and are still—manufactured in America and had revolutionized the commercial production of ice cream. When Frank inquired as to why this influx of production equipment was occurring, a wizened Bengali trader wiped his brow with a tattered handkerchief and told him to look around.

"This is very hot country," he said. "There's a never-ending demand for ice cream."

Italians cling to a stubborn, prideful ownership of the

production of gelato vis-à-vis a certain subset of proprietary domestic gelato machine manufactures such as Carpigiani and Cattabriga. Cardinal Craxi held the same prejudice; When he met Frank for an offsite pow wow at Giolitti, the famous gelateria near the Pantheon in Rome, he asserted that Italian gelato could only be produced from the inner chambers of these machines.

But Frank noted that the wide use of Emery Thompson freezers in the sub-Sahara was a recognition of their durability and superiority; and the overall growth in general of the dairy industry in Africa was an indication of exportable wealth. If he were an investing man—and of course, he was not—Cardinal Craxi controlled *la borsa*—Frank Bruno would bet on Kentucky Fried Chicken and Baskin Robbins in the sub-Sahara; not on McDonalds, not on Starbucks and not on Chipotle—nothing with heat. Craxi, however, could not get past the Emery Thompson conundrum. It baffled him. He was, after all, Italian, and he steadfastly believed that it was not possible to manufacture gelato with an American machine.

Ice cream is gelato and vice versa, Frank argued. World views on this and other matters in regard to dairy products had to change.

The matter of moving Babe's Canadian cash-stash and gold bars (all twenty Troy pounds of it) to Switzerland was a tactical problem and not a moral or ethical dilemma for Frank. Again, his restaurant training from the CIA—the ability to think and act on his feet—along with an understanding of international logistics from his training at the other CIA—came in handy in this matter. When something absolutely needs to get there overnight, and without a customs inspection, there is only one option—the United States Air Force.

Frank persuaded his mole at the Niagara Falls 914th Tactical Airlift Command to arrange for passage of his shipment for a few dollars more than the usual gift certificates he plied his operative with. He met the C-140 transport when it landed at Vicenza, threw the bubble wrapped air pack into the trunk of his rented Audi, and headed for the Brenner Pass. He was taking the long way to Lucerne.

Babe met him there a few days later with an imprimatur of Regina Ornella Carruana attached to her newly minted Swiss Bank account. It was after the money had been safely tucked away that she told Frank she was selling the restaurant to Bebe Lo Piccolo for the original offer amount of $450,000, structured slightly differently than the cancelled bank check, and with a closing date of next Friday. She would be returning soon to deposit the proceeds of the sale of the restaurant and she wondered if Frank might still be in Europe, and did he want to meet up?

"Babe," Frank said, marveling at this woman he had known all his life but who he seemed to know even less of now, "you're on your own."

Babe La Bruna was indeed alone at the second closing of the property formerly known as the Magaddino Funeral Home and presently called Restaurant Giuseppe Basi.

The first closing was a legal transaction, conducted by lawyers and bankers and duly notarized by an official representative of the County Clerk's office in Niagara County. The second, and more important, closing occurred at the restaurant and was attended only by Babe and Bebe Lo Piccolo.

"Let's do this in the room. I've got to see the room, first."

"Alright;" Babe said, "follow me."

They proceeded down the stairs, past the prep kitchen, through the walk-in cooler, into the walk-in freezer, moved the rolling racks, pushed the kick plate at the bottom of the cooler panel, and finally entered into the room.

"I knew it was here!" Lo Piccolo shrieked. "My old man talked about it all the time. He won his first ten Gs here in a card game. That ten Gs staked him in the business."

"Touching. Where's the cash?"

Lo Piccolo placed three envelopes on the table. Restaurateurs share a common bond. They live daily through the same travails, acquire the same habits, and most, not all, respectfully observe a moment of silence when a colleague is counting money. They know how important it is to do the job correctly, twice.

"I want a blow job," Lo Piccolo clamped down hard on Babe's wrist.

"Eat shit."

"I want a blow job or I'm walking away. This place is mine, legally."

Babe straightened up and laughed.

"That's one expensive blow job."

"That's what I want. I want to see you suck my cock. And if you don't, I've got Hook Nose out in the car. He can hack you up in no time. You'll be in the river by noon and nobody will find you for months. Everybody thinks you killed, Joe and got off on a technicality."

A restaurateur, even if he or she does not own their own building, can put a finger on everything that goes down on their premises. It's a sad, sad thing to walk out of your restaurant for the last time. What had seemed like an eternity—the work, the dirt, the hours, the mistakes, the simple pleasures, the goddamn customers—were all gone now. Finished. And it had all happened so quickly.

"Hand job," Babe countered.

"Blow job."

"Alright. I presume you took a shower this morning?"

"I lathered up just for you, Babe."

Babe got down on her knees. She was not about to leave any money on the table. This was her final exit strategy from the restaurant business.

"Wait a minute," Lo Piccolo pulled up. "There's no cameras in here?"

Babe reassured him there were none. But she did tilt

her head to the right, so that the camera—a throw-in as part of the new five-camera security system install, mounted from inside the ceiling tile—would capture every graphic detail of Lo Piccolo's spit shine. She planned on sending Trixie Lo Piccolo a very special Christmas greeting card this year from Switzerland.

TWENTY

"You pick the spot, Leonard. It's your call," Frank told Cousin Leonard who was now on the public dole officially and without any pretense. "I've been racking my brain for months trying to figure out where Joe's favorite spot was and I came to the conclusion he didn't have one. He was the life of the party wherever he went."

"How about the Gorge?"

"Perfect."

"I took Joe to my spot between Butterfly Rock and the Whirlpool. He loved it there. He didn't want to fish it. He just liked sitting on the rocks and watching the water rush by. I'll never forget the time he mooned a bunch of Canadian fishermen on the other side. They mooned us back."

The Gorge was, of course, the living reserve of the

southeastern march of Niagara Falls, a spectacular geological remnant of the Wisconsin glaciations composed essentially from Lockport dolostone, Rochester shale, and piteous sandstone.

It was not a canyon, which would imply a certain incomprehensibility to its grandeur juxtaposed to the subject matter of time and space; gorge was an appropriate word. It implied danger and intrigue but it was ultimately approachable and navigable by the sure-footed and the sober.

Ask any resident of Niagara Falls and they will acknowledge that indeed the Falls are majestic in their raw power. But it is the Gorge of Niagara that is infinitesimally more beautiful and sublime, telling the story of our human existence along its stratified layers of rock.

Frank and Cousin Leonard descended the Gorge by way of the Devil's Hole steps. It was at this very spot, in the year 1763, where a British detachment from Rogers' Rangers was overwhelmed and defeated by a Seneca ambush, resulting in the scalping of eighty-one heads and thereby sending a jolting message to British Commander Lord Jeffery Amherst that Pontiac's Rebellion was on.

Cousin Leonard was in his true element in the Gorge, even more so than in a commercial kitchen, and he bounded down the Devil's Hole stairs with his fishing pole and tackle box like an exuberant Labrador retriever.

Frank carried the last remains of Chef Joe Bass in

one hand, and a bottle of Ridge Montebello with the other. He was not a shore fisherman.

The last twenty feet or so saw them sliding down the embankment sideways, and landing amongst an outcropping of rocks next to the lower rapids of the Niagara River. They had made it to Cousin Leonard's spot.

"How do we do this?" Cousin Leonard asked. "I never done nothing like this before."

"We'll just play it by ear," Frank said.

They set Joe down on the rocks. Cousin Leonard started dressing his fishing pole and Frank cracked open the bottle of red wine and poured it into paper cups for them to drink. The sun had not yet come up but the sky showed promise.

Cousin Leonard was a magnificent shore fisherman and that's what it took to negotiate the lower Niagara River. The current rushed by so fast, and the rocks that lined the bottom of the river bed were so obstinate, that a less talented angler could easily get frustrated by the constant snag of the line. Fly fishermen thumb their noses at shore fishermen but not so here at Niagara. There was no wading in this body of water with your cutesy LL Bean fishing waders. Only the foolhardy waded into the lower Niagara River because if you were fortunate to get a strike, chances are you, and not the fish, were soon to become dead unless you had the leverage of the earth to rely upon.

Cousin Leonard fished for hours, landing a twenty-three pound Coho salmon and an eighteen-pound lake trout, all without losing a single lure on the rocks. Frank sat back and watched the sun rise in the sky.

"Can we just do nothing?" Cousin Leonard finally said, when he pulled his line out of the water for the last time of the day.

"How so?"

"I mean can we just leave Joe down here? Look, I want to put him against these two rocks, down in this little crevice, out of the wind. Nobody comes here, anyways. It's my spot. Everybody goes over to where the power plant is or further up along the shore. It's so easy to catch something there. They're all afraid of the rocks here. But, I tell you, I've fished this spot my whole life, and I know this is where the salmon spawn."

"We can do anything you want, Cousin Leonard."

"Good," he said. "I want to keep Joe here where I can find him. I want to come back here every time and tell him how sorry I am."

Food Companion

This remains the only surviving printed copy of the menu at Restaurant Giuseppe Basi besides the countless others tucked away in the back of desk drawers from competing restaurants and restaurant owners, clumsily referred to in industry parlance as restaurateurs—a puckish word if ever there was one—imparting a sense of illegitimacy and incompetence to the profession of food service.

Menus were frequently pilfered from the hostess station by other chefs and spies—a confluence of local *'Ndrangheta* (friends-of-friends), visiting culinary professionals, tourists, and locals. Replacement copies were issued only after the coffee and wine stains of those menus remaining in circulation became so controversial as to provoke an argument between Babe and Chef over their appearance.

The particular menu in question was produced on

an IBM Selectric typewriter, most probably in 1996. Restaurant Giuseppe Basi historians agree that 1996 was the year Chef Joe Bass began saucing the ravioli dish with butter and sage after a food critic side-swiped him in a review with the complaint that too many of the pasta offerings featured variations of the famous house salsa di pomodoro as the accompaniment.

Babe and the service staff took the side of the food critic on this issue. Chef fulminated for three days and then finally agreed to concessions.

The typist for all printed editions of the menu was Gloria Basi. She transcribed every iteration of her son's near-illegible handwriting while working as a secretary for the Carborundum Abrasives Company's Silicon and Fine Powders division. It was manufactured on legal-size cardstock and secretly photocopied on early Saturday mornings when Gloria entered the factory building through the security entrance under false pretense. Her signature was time-stamped at the desk and she was allowed to pass through, after informing the rental cop that she was going into the administrative quarters to "tidy up her desk."

Considerations

Chef gave little credence to the need for documentation of his recipes. His métier was strictly a spoken language—intelligible to his immediate staff and, of course, to his mother, who was tasked with the burden of writing the menu itself.

There were practical explanations as to why Chef never bothered to record his recipes. For starters, he was paranoid and semi-literate. His roundsman, Cousin Leonard, was completely illiterate and lacking in judgment. But Frank Bruno's arrival ushered in a new approach to the back of the house at Restaurant Giuseppe Basi. He likened his situation to that of a National Geographic linguist sent into the bush to attempt to preserve a near-extinct language from the few remaining tribesmen.

Recipe standardization is a maddening affair—fraught with incomplete information, missed steps, unreliable yields, and shaky food cost assumptions. Frank Bruno plowed forward in those early dark days with pen and legal pad in hand, shadowing Cousin Leonard from station to station.

He started with the house bread and then moved to the pasta section as that is where he would be spending the majority of his time cooking. He was determined to get some numbers down on paper. Putting an ounce-count or measure of weight next to an ingredient set was the only way Frank could make sense of what had transpired in Chef's kitchen. It had once bustled with the promise of greatness but now remained frozen shut like the prairies of Manitoba.

Easier said than done.

Nearly every time Frank thought he had a complete recipe and ingredient set, Cousin Leonard would add a new twist that further delayed his attempt to distill the process into logical steps. He gave up after only four attempts. He simply ran out of time. And besides, the restaurant got busy again.

"Now, why didn't you tell me about the anchovies in the San Giuseppe?" Frank scolded Cousin Leonard for his erratic methods.

"Because you didn't ask."

Menu – Restaurant Giuseppe Basi
circa 1996

Minestre

Zuppa alla Strachiatella
Minestra di Zucchine
Pasta e Fusari

Anitpasti

Antipasto di Verdure
Affetato di Salumi
Mozzarella di Casa
Calamari Fritti
Parmigiano delle Vacche Rosse

Primi

Spaghettini Picante al Prezzemolo
Linguine alle Vongole
Rigatoni al Ragu
Tornarelli Cacio e Pepi
Fusilli alla Calabrese
Gnocchi di Patate
Gnocchi di Ricotta
Ravioli Burro e Salvia
Pappardelle al Ragu di Coniglio
Lasagnette del San Giuseppe

Secondi

Pesce all'Acqua Pazzo
Filleto di Manzo
Pollo alla Brace
Roast Beef

Contorni
Insalata verde
Insalata mista
Spinaci al Burro
Patate

Pane Casareccio –
Provolone cubes and 'Nduja

American Supper Menu
Cream of Tomato Soup
Celery, Olives, Radishes, Hard Boiled Egg
Shrimp Cocktail
Sardines and Crackers
Egg Foo Yung

Entrees
Deluxe Hamburger and French Fries
Liver with Bacon
Leftover Cold Chicken Platter
Lamb Chops
NY Strip Steak

Bread Butter and Pickles

Pane Casareccio

Ingredients

- 37 ½ lb. bread flour
- 9 oz. salt
- 3 oz. yeast
- 7 ½ oz. sugar
- 7 ½ oz. milk powder
- 29 ¼ lb. water

Methods

Add water, salt, sugar, milk powder to bowl

Add flour, yeast

Mix on 1st speed 3-4 minutes

Mix on 2nd speed 3-4 minutes until dough comes away loosely from side of bowl.

Take temp and record.

Refrigerate overnight in bulk.

Next day, remove from bin.

Divide.

Rest on bench with semolina.

Shape into loaves.

Proof on boards.

Bake for 40 minutes, no steam.

Description

The bread should be shaped into an elongated *batard* and scored down the center line so that it blooms fully to both sides. Since the dough is very wet, be sure to use generous amounts of semolina while handling and proofing it.

Notes

Restaurant Giuseppe Basi charged for bread. This practice, instituted by Chef, was met with disbelief and outrage, and prompted mass walk-outs during the early days of service, much to the chagrin of Babe La Bruna, who had to deal the storm of protest from those who had never heard of such a thing.

Chef mischievously popped his head from the kitchen door when these early outbursts occurred. His plan was working. It was a clear shot across the bow to his future audience; that if you wanted to eat in this restaurant, you will pay for your bread.

It was Chef's way or the highway.

But Babe bore the brunt of the abuse. Chef began cutting small cubes of Provolone to accompany his bread basket and added a tiny schmear of 'Nduja—a spicy, Calabrian preserved pork product not bound by casing—on a monkey dish set next to the bread.

This was how Restaurant Giuseppe Basi came upon its signature *amuse-bouche*, although Chef was hesitant to refer to in such terminology, believing he did not have the chops to pull off any public displays of French. He did, however, admire the premise of the *amuse-bouche*. Chef wanted the Provolone's dry saltiness to overwhelm one's salivary glands immediately, lubricated by the fat of the 'Nduja and the crumb of the bread which brought instant relief from the oppressive sting of the Provolone.

It worked so well that the restaurant developed an unforeseen complication—bread squatters. These were the customers that came in to indulge solely on the restaurant's bread service and drink glasses of tap water.

Touché, Chef thought.

He had wanted to make a point; the point being that the value of bread is priceless, artificially supported by governments to feed their populations, but at the expense of the baker who must rise long before anyone else and toil on impossibly thin margins to continue the profession.

Chef added a hefty room fee to any suspected bread squatter's bill, and that put an end to that.

Spaghettini Picante Al Prezzemolo

Ingredients

- ¼ cup olive oil
- ¼ cup colatura di alici
- 4 sm. red chili peppers, diced fine
- 2 bunch Italian parsley, rough chopped
- 1 sm. lemon, rind of zested
- 8 oz. parsley pesto, divide over plates and dollop
- 1 ea. salt to taste, needs salt
- 1 lb. spaghettini, dry pasta
- Parmesan cheese, grated tableside
- 2 oz. red chili flakes

Methods

Prepare the "sauce" in Robot Coupe by using parsley, lemon zest, red chili flakes, Parmesan cheese, and pepper; and drizzle in the colatura di alici. The mixture should be wet but not runny. Taste. Set aside.

In sauté pan, meld olive oil and diced hot pepper. Hit pan with pasta water or stock, whichever you prefer, but make sure there is enough of a liquid base to toss the pasta so that it does not dry out.

Incorporate cooked pasta with tongs. Remove from heat, add parsley sauce, and mix thoroughly. Do not add parsley sauce while pan is over open flame, as it will distort the color of the "pesto." Divide among serving bowls and drizzle additional amount of colatura di alici over top.

Plate in shallow bowls. Grate cheese table side. Serve with monkey dish of preserved hot peppers in olive oil.

Description

The dish should appear slightly mounded in the center of the serving bowl; make sure there is at least a circular inch of clean porcelain showing from the beginning of its curvature. The overall desired effect is to provide a clean and uncomplicated taste. Failure to clean the parsley properly before making the pesto is the one true way to fuck up this dish. The flat leaf of the parsley and the stem should both be used.

Notes

At first, diners did not know what to make of this simple dish, and it was ignored for a long time.

"Spaghettini and parsley. You've got to be kidding."

Chef refused to take it off the menu or add anything that might sex it up, such as a protein source that would allow him to charge more. Finally, Babe instructed the servers to explain it to the customers as a variation on pesto, a term that rankled Chef, but one which proved inspiring, and resulted in steady sales.

Records indicate that it was a mid-week dish, ordered mostly by local regulars—women on diets—as the primi course followed by Pesce all'Acqua Pazzo, or as a default recommendation by servers to the pain-in-the-ass vegetarian crowd.

It pleased Chef to see the dish go out in all of its unadorned glory. It pleased him greatly.

Pasta e Fusari

Ingredients

- 24 oz. pork stock
- ¾ lb. canneroni lisci
- ½ lb. fagioli borlotti
- 1 ea. white onion
- 1 med. potato
- 4 oz. olive oil
- 2 oz. salt
- 3 oz. pepper
- 3 oz. Good Seasons Italian seasoning mix

Methods

Soak the borlotti beans in two changes of fresh water overnight, then drain. In clay pot, combine beans and pork stock (including unsmoked ham hock), bring to boil, then bake until beans are done—with a firm texture but creamy on inside. Reserve separately the pork broth and the beans. Do not discard the broth.

Peel and set aside one cooked potato.

Sauté onion in saucepan with olive oil. Add cooked beans and cubed potato to saucepan. Add pork broth until beans are just covered and cook additional 30 minutes.

Remove half of the beans and pass through a food mill back into the sauce pan. Add additional pork broth, and reduce until liquid has nearly evaporated.

Cook canneroni lisci and reserve.

Now, add dry Good Seasons Italian to saucepan

with bean mixture; freshen with a small amount of stock. Stir to incorporate, and add olive oil, salt and pepper. Taste.

Add cooked pasta and mixed together. Divide among bowls. Grind black pepper over top and drizzle with additional olive oil.

Notes

The Pasta e Fusari served at Restaurant Giuseppe Basi was developed to meet the peculiar dietary requirements of Alberto Fanfani, a regular who dined at the bar most every night while reading the newspapers and downing two shots of Canadian whiskey, and who named the traditional Pasta & Fagioli in the regional dialect of his birthplace, Roccaromana, Campania.

Fanfani's diet was a strict one. He breakfasted on Cheerios with a raw egg beaten into the milk. Lunch consisted of a sandwich. Dinner, six days a week, called for Pasta e Fusari, but not a soupy mess of a Pasta Fagioli. Instead, the dish was to be threadbare and dry, like Alberto Fanfani himself. He dictated the preparation to Chef, who upon rendering it the first time, declared his trademark catchphrase to be used later on his Food Network show.

"This meal is a disaster area."

Chef frantically tried to doctor the Pasta e Fasuri before sending it out for the first time. He looked up at his pantry shelving and spotted a sample of Good Seasons Dry Italian mix left by a salesman. Chef had treated the salesman rather cruelly, belittling his pronunciation of his catalog of Italian specialties, and now he felt great remorse for his caustic ways and vowed to call the salesman the next day and apologize.

He never did. Chef did something more musical to the ears of a salesman. He put in an order.

Fanfani was so beguiled by the Pasta e Fusari that he dined on it every night for the next six years, until he passed away at the age of eighty-eight. In that time, he banged more cocktail waitresses from the perch of his bar stool, second-in from the server drink pick-up. His robustness in bed was the stuff of legend, attributed not to any prescription drugs, but to the workings of Chef's Pasta e Fusari.

Fanfani bequeathed a gift of $50,000 in his last will and testament to the restaurant, which allowed Chef to finish his dream prep kitchen in the basement. That was where Chef stored his Good Seasons Italian mix, obtained discreetly from the salesman he had once berated, but who now depended upon the commission from the account of Restaurant Giuseppe Basi to put his daughter through college.

Lasagnette al San Giuseppe

Ingredients

- 12 oz. fresh pasta—cut into strips 12 mm wide
- 5 oz. veal meat balls, scooped in 1 oz. servings
- 8 oz. Salsa di Pomodoro
- 4 oz. ricotta
- 2 oz. Romano

Methods

The success of the dish depends upon the success of the four components—pasta, sauce, ricotta, and meatballs. Chef made each of these separately on a regular basis. It was yet another example of how repetition yielded an advantage in professional cooking.

The fresh pasta was sheeted into 12-millimeter strips with the aid of a pasta machine attachment. The strips dried for a day, on parchment-lined sheet pans dusted with semolina, in the basement prep kitchen, and were cooked to order.

The veal meatballs were made from a mixture of ground veal, soaked stale bread, ground almond, anchovy, salt, pepper, egg, parsley, and Romano. They were portioned with a 1 ounce scoop, fried in olive oil in a cast iron pan, and then set on another sheet pan while reserved for service.

The ricotta was the byproduct of the fresh mozzarella-making process; a whey mixture yielding a grainy variety of the cheese, with a coarseness Chef preferred to the fresh milk method.

Description

Lasagnette al San Giuseppe is served in a boat-style baking dish of the common variety found in diners. The fresh cooked pasta is sauced in the sauté pan, then tonged onto the baking dish. The meatballs are placed strategically amongst the coated noodles. The Romano is then dusted to form a calcium adhesive for the dollops of ricotta that are piped into the dish, similar to practice of caulking. It is then baked for five minutes at 500 degrees. The dish is then placed into the salamander broiler for a final scorching, until a hint of crust developed on the ricotta.

Notes

There is a beginning, but there is no end, to the preparation of a lasagna.

Chef knew that he wanted to put his namesake lasagna onto the menu, but that it would not sell in its traditional form. He also did not want to batch size and cook it ahead of time, as most lasagnas are done, since this approach would serve to dehydrate his prized fresh ricotta.

It was a rare instance in which Chef turned against tradition and judgment, and decided to assemble the dish *à la minute,* first in a sauté pan, then into a baking dish, and finished for a moment in the salamander.

By doing this, he could ensure a proper ratio of pasta-to-meatball-to-ricotta-to-sauce, all in the blink of an eye. Otherwise, why not just batch size it, set up a hot table, open an all-you-can-eat buffet, and let the cows graze?

Chef once listened to an enthusiastic server explain that the dish was not a traditional lasagna, or even a traditional Lasagnette al San Giuseppe, but a deconstructed version of the classic. He pulled the server aside, regarded her bosom, refrained in moment of better judgment from commenting on her endowment, and gently, very gently, presented her this argument:

"There is beginning, but there can be no end to lasagna. We do not deconstruct in this kitchen. The dish stands on its own. It sells and sells. Therefore, we prep, and we prep for the next shift. That's why putting lasagna onto the menu was such a difficult choice. You think we are happy that it sells, but the plain truth is that all chefs want their dishes to go to a cold place and die, so we can all go home and get some rest. Lasagna always sells, and always requires us to do more work, even when we are exhausted, and therefore we despise its very existence."

About the Author

In late 2007, Vincent McConeghy was faced with the sudden and inexplicable prospect of closing his artisan bread bakery (a fourteen-year-old enterprise) due to unprecedented price shocks occurring in the wheat futures market.

What McConeghy and others in the food business did not realize at the time was that they were the front line recipients of the effects of a totally new phenomena in food markets and high finance—the indexing of food commodities by major Wall Street firms.

Some Wall Street firms had figured out a way to game the system, and with the deep pockets of sovereign wealth funds, rained down a global economic maelstrom that preceded the great financial collapse of 2008, and whose brunt was borne by small businesses such as McConeghy's and thousands of others.

"I did not understand how this could happen," McConeghy said. "We were the tiniest speck in the entire supply chain—the small business end-user. The price of bread can only rise to meet supply costs to a point. Governments understand this. In many countries, they subsidize the price of wheat because it stabilizes populations. But not in the US, and many small businesses here faced extinction if they did not react quickly."

Fast forward to 2010, signs of another food crisis loomed on the horizon, and the role of Wall Street firms in commodity manipulation has become better understood—if not completely agreed upon—and debated fiercely within many financial circles.

This gaming of the commoditization of food provided impetus to McConeghy's development of Gastro Detective and its main character, Frank Bruno. In doing so, McConeghy created a new sub-genre for the fiction thriller category—the Resto Thriller—where food, finance, global politics and the recurring drama of the restaurant business collide with dramatic and unexpected consequences.

"Food is one of the most heavily reported upon subjects, whether by traditional media and publishing outlets, or by thousands of blogs that cover every nuance of the industry. Gastro Detective is my attempt to carve a niche for the discussion of food and service in the fictional sense. Simply put, Gastro Detective is a Resto-Thriller; it's not about food, per se, but about our struggle to feed ourselves in thoroughly modern way."

Visit the website for *Gastro Detective* at GastroDetective.com.